3/16

In an underground apartment building "twilight souls" inhabit the space between life and death. Interwoven with their stories are those of inhabitants of the living world: a retired sea captain, a psychotic former child actor (possibly the sea captain's illegitimate son?), and the technicians who monitor the Burrow, making sure its occupants have a constant supply of oxygen and food. Through all of their stories, and the ways in which their lives, past and present, intertwine, Jim Krusoe creates a surprisingly poignant picture of life, what remains when we die, and the interconnection of all experience.

# PRAISE FOR *THE SLEEP GARDEN*

"*The Sleep Garden* is Jim Krusoe's looniest and most satisfying book. Inane and trivial questions are given close consideration, while questions of life and death (and the differences between life and death) are intimated and then suspended.

Only a special kind of genius (or an idiot savant, as the book suggests) could dream this stuff up. I have no idea how he does it, but do it he does, and no one else can blur stupidity and significance with such sublime, funny, and human results."

—MICHAEL SILVERBLATT, *Bookworm* KCRW

# PRAISE FOR JIM KRUSOE

"Krusoe's sure and subtle imaginings of such characters—yearning, isolated and finally enigmatic—place him among the foremost creators of surreal Americana."

—*The New York Times Book Review*

"Krusoe's latest is a self-reflective coming-of-age story wrapped in a fable and sprinkled with wry observations . . . *Parsifal* becomes a piquant commentary on tensions between nostalgia and reality, the past and the present, and humanity's need for myths."

—*Publishers Weekly*

"Jim Krusoe is the mad scientist, the man behind the curtain . . . Krusoe does something magical with regular words and regular life. His adjectives glow with possibility . . . like an alien presence with a new language that sounds enough like our own to make us strain to uncover its meaning."

—*Los Angeles Times*

"Jim Krusoe's work is full of the most curious urgency: I love to keep reading, and I don't know what I'm waiting for, exactly, but I know whatever I find will hover in my peripheral vision for a while after I'm done."

—AIMEE BENDER, author of *The Color Master*

# the
# SLEEP
# GARDEN

# the SLEEP GARDEN

## JIM KRUSOE

Tin House Books
Portland, Oregon & Brooklyn, New York

Published by Tin House Books, Portland, Oregon, and Brooklyn, New York

Distributed by W. W. Norton and Company


Library of Congress Cataloging-in-Publication Data

Krusoe, James.
  The sleep garden / Jim Krusoe. -- First U.S. edition.
    pages ; cm
  ISBN 978-1-941040-18-8 (alk. paper)
  I. Title.
  PS3561.R873S58 2016
  813'.54--dc23

                                  2015031246



First US Edition 2016
Printed in USA
Interior design by Diane Chonette
www.tinhouse.com

*In memory of Michael Woodcock*

There are nights when I awake from a terrible nightmare, my simplest and most frightening dream. I am lying in a deep sleep in the bed I lay down in that evening. The setting and the time are the same as the actual setting and time. If the nightmare begins at midnight, for instance, it places me in precisely the degree of darkness and silence reigning at that hour. I can see and feel my position; I know the bed and room I am sleeping in. My dream stretches like a fine skin over my body and over the state of my sleep at the moment. One might even say I am awake. I am awake though asleep and dreaming my wakefulness at the same moment I am dreaming my sleep.

— MAX BLECHER, *Adventures in Immediate Irreality* (trans. Michael Henry Heim)

Everyone that sleeps is beautiful, every thing in the dim light is beautiful ...

— WALT WHITMAN, "The Sleepers"

I

■

*Where are we?*
*How did we come here?*
*Where are we going?*

■

*And anyway, who lies sleeping here with us?*
*Wherever that is—*
*I mean—wherever we are.*

**II**

■

To begin: the Burrow is a low mound that rises out of the ground. It rests on what would be, if not for the Burrow itself, a vacant lot on the edge of town, though not the farthest edge. On one end of the lot, on the west side of the Burrow, and far enough away so there are no drainage problems, is a small pond. What kind of pond? Picture a body of water about the size of a supermarket parking lot, with stands of cattails, frogs, tadpoles, and such, plus various insects, both on the water and flying above it. This pond grows larger in spring and in summer shrinks to the size of, say, a convenience store parking lot. In the fall and winter it stays somewhere roughly between the two extremes. On its eastern shore is a tree, possibly a cypress, but possibly something else entirely. A sad fact about the people who live in this town is that nobody knows much of anything about the names of trees.

Still, like so many other things in the world, this particular burrow is more than its name implies. This burrow has people living in it. It has five or six tenants, depending on how many of its apartments are rented at any given time, because, as you probably guessed, the Burrow is really an apartment building, and although it isn't called "the Burrow" in any formal sense—it's never had any formal name at all—it was the Burrow's neighbors, the very same ones who can't seem to tell one tree from another, who called it that back when it was first constructed. So to this day, whether out of affection or derision, "the Burrow" is how people, including those who live inside it, refer to the place. And while it's true that some of the children in the neighborhood say the Burrow is scary, no one offers any specifics. It's the kind of place that children like to pretend is scary on principle. It's part of being a child, and certainly that doesn't stop those same children from playing in the pond next to it when school isn't in session, albeit giving the Burrow a glance from time to time to make sure there's nothing frightening rushing toward them from it as they play.

So picture a mound of dirt with things growing out of the top, plants, new shoots, weeds, but having a front door, and you are picturing the Burrow.

■

Meanwhile, inside the Burrow, Jeffery is thinking this: Suppose a person spent his whole life being way ahead of the curve, was überbrilliant, far in front of every other person in the world who was also working on whatever problem this first person was working on, so incredibly advanced, et cetera, et cetera, that those in his dust were totally blind to the fact there was even anyone out in front of them? They would look, of course, but all they would see was a big dust cloud, without having the slightest idea what was causing it. And correspondingly, when the genius, or whatever you want to call him, looked behind, and squinted through the dust of his own making, those others weren't visible.

But then, Jeffery thinks, one day, maybe thirty or forty years after this genius first embarked on his journey and the dust from the cloud settled, he happened to look back once again, and this time, because there wasn't any more dust at all, he could see for sure there was nobody following him. There was only an empty plain, or road, or stage, or whatever you want to call it. In other words, whoever had been back there trailing after him must have taken a whole different path, or several different paths. So there he was—wherever "there" was—completely alone. But here's the thing: out of all those people who, a long time ago, were working on the same idea as he was, nobody cared. Every one of them had moved on to other projects, much better and more timely ones, and as a result, the genius was not ahead of anyone anymore. He'd been totally forgotten and whatever he might have done, whatever he did, meant nothing. Zero.

And as for this supposed genius, what word would Jeffery use to describe him?

■

Jeffery is in his midthirties and has hair the color of untoasted whole-wheat sandwich bread. He's still in fairly good shape because he exercises every day—squats, sit-ups, push-ups—right next to his bed first thing every morning. Though he's starting to develop a little pot on his stomach, it's not unusual for his age. He tells himself he needs to lay off the starch, but hasn't gotten around to it. It's not that big a deal.

■

Also: in addition to the problem with identifying their trees, none of the town's inhabitants seem to be able to pronounce the name of their own town, St. Nils.

That is, they can and do pronounce it in one of two ways: Saint *Niles*, like the river, or *Nils*, which rhymes with *pills*, but it appears they have no idea which one is correct.

■

The fact is, it was Raymond who inspired this idea of the alleged genius-person-so-far-ahead-of-everyone-else to pop into Jeffery's head, and Jeffery's first Raymond-as-a-genius thought came when he was smack in the middle of Raymond's living room in the Burrow, sitting on Raymond's couch surrounded by a humongous number of decoys: on wall shelves, on tables, even lined up along the baseboards. Raymond had carved each one, and now, apparently, he waited for some mysterious future event to move them out of there. In addition to the finished decoys there were also several piles of lumber for future decoys. There were also open cans of paint leaking fumes and smelling up the place—not a bad smell, but, well . . . *paint*, and of course Raymond was living in the middle of all this.

Then Raymond sat down on the recliner opposite the couch and made it recline by means of a lever on one side. Next, he took off his right shoe, propped his right foot up on the part of the recliner that had turned into a little platform, and allowed his left foot, its shoe still on, to rest quietly on the rug.

So while it was clear that Raymond had a vision, Jeffery still had a hard time working out precisely what vision that might be.

Is he a genius or a complete idiot?

And, for that matter, what would you call Jeffery for thinking all of this?

■

And yet there *is* something troubling about the Burrow, something hard to name, maybe something about the low shadow it casts on the vacant lot around sunset, or maybe the smell of its walls after a November rain, so maybe the children—bless them— are right to keep their distance.

■

Because Raymond is a big guy, and gentle, and his head is big and gentle, too, with dark brown hair like burnt whole-wheat toast, and frizzy, the kind of hair a person might want to lean their own head against if he or she were tired, but if they did they would be disappointed because what they would be leaning on would be Raymond's skull, which is very hard. *As hard as a wooden decoy*, a person who leaned his or her head against it might be thinking.

∎

Meanwhile: outside the Burrow, new shoots of trees, new wood, reach out of the ground, toward air, toward sun, toward something they can't actually see, something they have no way to be sure is even there.

∎

What was Raymond's reaction to Jeffery's explanation of the dust cloud and the person making it? It was to settle deeper into his recliner and shut his eyes. Finally, after about five minutes, Raymond spoke. "Like jets," he said, and proceeded to peel a Band-Aid from his finger and stare at the cut underneath, which Jeffery thought probably came from making decoys—a sliver or a slip of the knife. The skin beneath the Band-Aid was pale and puckered, not like skin at all, but more like those Styrofoam pellets people use for packing.

"Are you okay?" Jeffery asked. "And what do you mean, 'like jets'?"

Raymond stuck the Band-Aid back where it was. "Like once upon a time," he said, "there must have been some crazy old aeronautical engineer somewhere who spent his whole life thinking as hard as he could about how to get propeller planes to speed up, maybe by making bigger propellers, or shorter wings, or both, or whatever it would take, and let's say that in the end he figured out exactly the way to do it; let's say that he increased the speed by fifty or a hundred miles an hour, which nobody ever imagined could be done by anybody, so the guy was a genius. But in the meantime, somebody else had invented jets."

"Oh," Jeffery said, because he had to give Raymond credit: the man, no matter what else he was, was full of surprises, and even after Madeline left him to be with Viktor, Raymond stayed friends with Jeffery.

Because it was also true that before Madeline left Raymond to be with Viktor, she left Jeffery to be with Raymond.

Which made the two of them buddies in a way. Losers.

The winner being Viktor, of course.

■

Though terms such as "winner" and "loser" are pretty much irrelevant in the Burrow.

■

Madeline also lives in the Burrow, as well as Heather and Viktor. There used to be another guy—Louis, his name was—but he moved out in the middle of the night awhile ago, and now his room is empty.

Maybe if they put a big sign out in front, Jeffery thinks, and officially called the building "The Burrow," then the place would be overrun with Middle Earth-o-philes, and the landlord, or whatever faceless real estate holding company actually owns this place, wouldn't be having this vacancy problem. On the other hand, is it his problem, or even a problem?

Does Jeffery really want to have to get to know a new tenant and then have to set boundaries with him or her?

■

On the other hand: Who was it among the Burrow's current crop of residents who called her fellow renters "a lonely, fucked-up group of individuals"?

That would be Madeline. She has red hair and once Viktor described her, correctly, as "a hot tamale."

■

*Tocar*: to touch.

■

Meaning the fur beneath and between the fingers, meaning the warmth of skin beneath the fur, the pulse of blood, the sleeping house of muscle, its patient throb against the hand, the hand connected to that which is the other, meaning the self outside the self, the self mysterious in the way we cannot ever be a mystery to ourselves, the self known through touching others in the way we ourselves can never be known, the self outside the self, of it being touched, of our being connected, for once not alone but a part, for once no different, for once at home in a world where we are never at home, for once ourselves, remembering, wherever we may be.

■

To the *St. Nils Eagle*

Dear Editors,

I have been noticing for quite a while various problems
associated with the use of firearms in this country. At
the same time I cannot ignore the fact that, with crime
rates being what they are, home protection is also an
issue. Today I am writing because I believe there is a
way to solve both problems at the same time. Namely,
people should give serious thought to requiring every
household in the land to have at least one crossbow
on its premises, both for sport and as a deterrent
factor. Here are the reasons I believe such legislation, if
enacted, might reverse the trends of death by firearms
and also the increasing dangers of home intrusions: 1)
To load a crossbow requires a fair amount of physical
strength, thus cutting down on any possibility of misuse
by children, old people, or invalids. 2) Crossbows, being
made of wood, are ecologically superior, and certainly
do not carry with them the stigmata of cop-killer
bullets and the discharge of poisonous gases or lead
into the atmosphere. 3) The time it takes to pull back
the string, and then to put an arrow (or bolt) in place,
while not long, can provide a much-needed "cooling

off" period in cases of a disagreement or domestic violence situations. 4) When necessary, they are deadly.

Yours truly,
A Sportsman

∎

Many residents of the neighborhood say the Burrow has its origin in the Cold War, or even earlier, during the Second World War. Purportedly, the government built it back then as a secret place to hide officials if the fighting got too close. But to counter that theory: Why would the government build a place like that for only six people? And which six could they have been?

Others say that the Burrow has its origin in some sort of geological formation, a swelling in the earth that the builders simply used to make their job easier, digging down, in the natural direction of gravity, instead of building unnaturally upward. Then they installed plumbing, ran electrical lines, and plastered over walls of dirt. It is cool in summer, people say, and warm in winter, and they are right.

But there are still others who contend that the Burrow is not that old at all. They posit that its origin was as the entrance of a tunnel dug to smuggle drugs, or possibly humans—though from where to where is never specified. In any case, this faction claims that someone, probably a relative of one of the agents who exposed the operation, bought the vacant lot cheap, then took advantage of the considerable improvements that had already been made by the crime lords, and turned it into its present configuration of underground apartments, renting them out at an exceedingly reasonable rate.

Clearly, this is a lot of speculation by a group of people who can't even bother to learn the names of their own trees. At the same time however, everyone agrees that one benefit to living there is that, possibly because the presence of the Burrow does not exactly announce itself to any criminal type, there has never been a break-in or a burglary in all the years of its existence. In other words, the Burrow is safe, and no matter what individual complaints its residents may have, they report feeling protected from the kind of harm they have felt in the places they lived before they arrived at the Burrow.

■

*Crossbows?*

■

It has been many years since the Captain was at sea, expertly piloting his giant ocean liner, the *Valhalla Queen*, in and out of fjords as contented passengers lined its decks to snap photos of icebergs, glaciers, and baby seals before racing inside to the ship's dining room to wolf down their sixth or seventh gourmet buffet of the day. *Worthless, degenerate swine*, the Captain used to mutter into the sleeve of his handsome dark-blue uniform, taking care that no one heard him. Then, as often as not, following his dinner at "The Captain's Table," the Captain hurried to the simple good taste of his own cabin, where he removed his jacket, stood in front of the bathroom mirror, put two fingers down his throat, and regurgitated everything into one of the black plastic bags he kept for that very purpose beneath his sink. When he finished, he'd rinse his mouth, replace his jacket, and carry the bag back outside, where he would nod at the various happy passengers who sat on deck chairs wrapped in blankets, staring stupidly at the Northern Lights as they awaited the midnight buffet to be set out in the second dining room. When he was certain he was totally alone, he'd hurl his former dinner as far away from the ship as he could, into the icy water, return to his cabin, and enjoy a dreamless sleep.

The Captain's hair is white these days, but above his left eye there is still a stain: a birthmark in the shape of an anchor. He combs his hair over it, and so successful is this strategy that even people who have known him for years are unaware of its existence.

■

Sometimes the residents of the Burrow will ask each other about the pond or the tree that hangs over it.

"How does the tree look to you these days? Does it look healthy? Do you ever wonder what kind of tree it is, exactly?"

Or, "How deep is the pond these days?" Or, "Have the birds begun to build their nests in the rushes of the pond?"

And the answer will invariably come back: "Actually, it's been awhile since I've been outside at all."

■

Jeffery thinks that out of everyone who lives at the Burrow, Raymond is the wild card. And as if to demonstrate this truth, on the very day following their conversation regarding jet planes, just as Jeffery is about to grasp the knob of the front door of the Burrow to go outside, who should appear but Raymond, his arms spread, grabbing on to the sleeve of Jeffery's tan, cotton-polyester, lightweight jacket.

"Jeffery," Raymond asks, "do you remember your dreams?"

Even from Raymond, this is a strange question. But then, what strikes Jeffery as even more bizarre is that Raymond must have been lurking by the front door for God knows how long, like the Ancient Mariner, waiting for him. And, what is even stranger, it is clear to Jeffery that Raymond must have gone to the door directly from his bed, because he is still wearing his red-and-white-striped pajamas, which could use a wash. Truly.

Also, there are three or four fresh wood shavings in his hair, as usual.

■

Raymond, being the Burrow's longest resident, is the one who remembers Louis best, and when Louis left suddenly, in the middle of the night, without an explanation, it made Raymond nervous. How could someone be there one moment and then in the next disappear? When Raymond tries to picture Louis now, he can only recall a tall, coffee-colored man with gray, curly hair who was fond of sweaters, and always polite, and who never failed to clean up after himself when he used the kitchen. But what else? He used to like to talk to Louis, he knows this, but what did the two of them ever talk about? What were Louis's features? What happened to him? The man seems to have been washed away somehow, and the thing that sticks most in Raymond's mind is, of all things, the sound of his name, *Louis*, which, curiously, was the same sound made by Louis's worn brown leather slippers as he shuffled down the hall on his way to the kitchen. At any rate, with Heather in her room most of the time and Viktor being with Madeline these days, that pretty much leaves only Jeffery for Raymond to talk to.

No wonder he misses Louis.

■

Viktor's favorite word is *rectum*. There are others that come close—*rector*, *correct*, *erect*, even *rectitude*—but for all-round satisfaction and simple purity of sound, *rectum* wins, hands down. *Rectum*, that great two-stroke gong of a word, beginning with the crispness of the *rec*, and then, just as the listener is brought to attention by the *rec*, comes the hollow *tum* of doom at the end: rec-tum, the whole journey of life in two syllables, and the end of life, too, if you think about it. And just guess where that exit point is? Garbage in/garbage out. People write all the time they ♥ something, so why isn't there an equivalent for the rectum? It is literally amazing that here we have one of the most important organs in the whole human body, and yet most people refuse to give it the recognition it deserves, have failed to embrace the power of this simple word. But Viktor has embraced it. That's his secret.

■

Meanwhile, Jeffery still has his hand on the knob of the Burrow's dark front door, getting ready to leave. "Why do you ask?" he asks Raymond.

"Because," Raymond answers, "I've been having the same bad dream lately, and I can't seem to stop it."

"Maybe you should write it down so you can re-member it," Jeffery says, and gestures toward the exit.

"I already remember it," Raymond replies. Somewhat disconcertingly, he begins to tug harder on the sleeve of Jeffery's jacket. It's one Jeffery was given several years ago by an old girlfriend, and for that reason it is his favorite article of clothing. It still smells of her patchouli and, at least in his mind, of her spit, which would sweetly leak from her mouth like a child's when she fell asleep on long rides, her head on his shoulder as he drove carefully homeward so as not to wake her. Her name was Pam, he thinks, or Jan.

"Okay," Jeffery surrenders. "Let's go to my apartment. You can talk about it there."

■

And what kind of town is it where people are so backward that they refuse to learn the names of the trees that are in their own neighborhood?

*Cypress or pine*—these careless people answer if you should ask them—*what difference does it make, as long as they are there?*

But aren't the names of things important?

The Burrow, for one.

■

"Twilight souls" is the name the Captain gives to the uncomplicated and unaware primitive races he came into contact with during his days on the high seas, caught, as they were, somewhere between animals and a higher being. But caught *where* exactly, the Captain refuses to specify.

■

*And where are we now?*
*How did we come to be here?*
*Where we going?*
*And anyway, do we even need to know?*

III

■

Madeline is looking in the mirror trying to decide whether she should pluck her eyebrows or just leave them alone. On the pro side it would give her something to do, and she's pretty bored, but on the con side she likes them the way they are. And there she is: red hair, full eyebrows, nice features though a little large, not like those mousey ones of Heather, which is good. So why doesn't she get more respect? She gets men following after her, sure, but respect—that's another matter entirely. On the other hand, who in the Burrow is capable of providing it? Raymond is, well . . . Raymond, and the word would never even cross his mind. Jeffery is old news and Viktor is intense—she'll give him that—but the only thing he comes close to respecting is money.

One of these days she's going to have to take her act on the road and get out of here before it kills her, but first she'd better figure out exactly what her act is going to be. Singing? No, though she has a nice enough voice. Dancing? Unfortunately not. Painting? Sculpture? Poetry? Nope, nope, and nope. The only thing she's at all good at is cooking, so maybe that will be it, she thinks. Stranger things have happened, that's for sure.

■

"In my dream," Raymond announces to Jeffery when they finally arrive at Jeffery's apartment, "I'm a duck, and my arms—or wings, I guess—are getting tired because I've been flying for days. Don't ask me how I know this. And not only have I been flying nearly forever, but the weather is incredibly bad—snow, sleet, hail, and fog, too—so I can barely see the ground below. Anyway, I ask the leader of the ducks—we have a leader—'Please, can we stop here?' but he says no.

"Then I say, 'How much longer?' but the leader, who's another duck, naturally, says I have to hang on. 'We're almost there,' he yells over the wind to me, but at the same time, Jeffery, I'm telling you, my arms really, really hurt. I mean, I can barely move them, and it feels like I'm starting to lose altitude."

Jeffery looks at him. The man is a little out of breath and his forehead is sweating. "That's some dream," he answers. "I can see why you'd remember it. But the fact is, Raymond, I was just on my way outside when you insisted on stopping me."

"But wait," Raymond goes on. "Just as I'm positive I'm going to drop into the ocean or into whatever it is that's below me—did I mention there are a lot of clouds, so it's impossible to see the ground at all?—the clouds separate, and there is the most beautiful pond I can imagine—cattails, and duckweed, and frogs—it's sort of like the one outside this place, and perfect for landing. And it turns out, in my dream anyway, that somehow I knew this exact place would be here all along; don't ask me how—instinct or something. Then, even better, guess who is flying right next to me? It's Madeline—who is also a duck, but still the same Madeline you and I both know, the one who left you for me (sorry) and then me for Viktor—and I tell her, 'Madeline, look. Other ducks are already down there; it will be great. We'll get a bite to eat, and maybe exchange some information about weather conditions and so on and so forth. We can make new friends, but don't you go getting too friendly, if you know what I mean, and Madeline kind of nods because her arms are busy flapping.

"So there we are, all of us gliding down to join the other ducks and, just as I'm thinking how great it feels not to have to move my arms—which are *so* tired—anymore, what do I hear but loud noises? (Well, I can't be positive how loud the noises are, scientifically speaking, because, as you know, a duck's ears aren't designed for picking up sounds—but I can tell you they are loud to me.) And then I can't move my arms at all; I'm falling, and everything gets dark."

Raymond's face suddenly goes flat and spongy, but like a sponge that isn't filled with water but with something else, something alien and scary. "Do you think this means I died?"

"I have no idea," Jeffery answers, because right in the middle of listening to Raymond talk about his dream, he found himself wishing for about the thousandth time that he had taped those episodes of his favorite old television sitcom, *Mellow Valley*. There were only seven of them, and he promised himself he'd do it before moving to the Burrow, but then other things got in his way.

■

Jeffery's apartment, like every apartment in the Burrow, consists of a study, a bedroom, and a bath. There is no kitchen, not even a hot plate, because down the hall is a real kitchen that everyone shares with surprisingly few complications of a territorial nature. Food arrives, is put away, is consumed. That's about it.

When he moved into the Burrow, his apartment came furnished: a bed, a brown leather couch, two lamps, a dresser, and two mismatched but comfortable chairs. Someone said the Burrow had been outfitted when a used furniture store caught fire, and most of the furniture was put outside for an impromptu sale even as the firemen were still shooting water on the blaze, trying (and failing) to save the building. Sometimes, if he's lying on the couch, his head pushed deep into one of its cushions, Jeffery believes he can detect the faintest tang of smoke and imagines he can hear the hiss of steam.

Above his couch Jeffery has tacked a photo from a sports magazine he found in the Burrow kitchen one day, piled on top of the trash. The picture is of a woman on her back on a straw mat. Her arms are at her sides, palms facing up, and her reddish-brown hair is spread out behind her. Her eyes are shut, and although she wears a light-blue two-piece bathing suit that allows the viewer to appreciate the gentle, but not ostentatious, swelling of her breasts, the breathtaking curve of her waist, the discreet in-scoop of her navel, there is nothing base or prurient about her. Instead, she is chaste and self-contained. She could be a wandering goddess taking a little time out to soak up some rays.

Meanwhile, the woman in the poster's shut eyes are saying—and not only to the person who snapped this photo in the first place, but now to Jeffery as well—"I don't recognize you. I could open my eyes right now, and still you wouldn't exist for me any more than if you never had been born. So move, asshole, because you are blocking my sunlight." And weirdly, it was this very poster Jeffery had been staring at when it occurred to him to take a stroll outside and check things out and maybe catch a little sun for a change, that is, before Raymond stopped him at the door.

■

It probably is no coincidence that the woman in the poster resembles Madeline.

■

Who was it that said: "The entire course of human history can basically be reduced to the acts of one total psychopath after another"?

■

So picture a boy, an average-looking boy, who has the usual childhood diseases—croup, flu, strep—and takes them all in stride or even better because he's a healthy kid, and what keeps his schoolmates in bed a week Junior will get over in a day. His mind, though, is another matter, because for one thing, he likes to cut up worms—lots of worms—in order to watch them writhe even though they lack faces to express their pain. He likes burning bugs, too, burning them with magnifying lenses so it takes awhile, and even though it's true they do have faces, small ones, still they can't change their expressions. Thank God for gasoline and rats. For the first time this boy can finally see what pain feels like outside of himself, which is the point, because this boy is not cruel; Junior is not a sadist, no. All Junior is looking for is someone—okay, *something*—he can share, compare notes with, to validate—though he would never use such a fancy word—his feelings. Anyway, there is a chance this boy, Junior, will grow out of this in time.

■

And it isn't until a whole day passes, or maybe two days, that Jeffery realizes he hasn't actually been outside at all since Raymond interrupted him with his stupid dream.

But then that's not so unusual, because Jeffery is always meaning to do things he never gets around to actually doing. Taping those episodes of *Mellow Valley*, for one thing.

Figuring out a way to be successful, for another.

■

Back in the days when he was in command of the *Valhalla Queen*, on some afternoons the Captain would walk out on deck in between buffets, carrying his favorite pistol, the Walther that had been a present from his father, Klaus Senior. Once a crowd had gathered, he would take a little target practice at whatever happened to be bobbing near the ship that day: birds, kelp, fishing-net floats, baby seals—whatever. His ritual was this: six rounds, no more, no fewer, never missing once. When he finally lowered his pistol after his last bullet blew to pieces some hapless arctic tern or plain-old seagull, his first mate would shout, "Hooray for the Captain. Another perfect score." And so the passengers would cheer as well, in the mistaken belief that there might somehow be a correlation between having a captain who was an excellent marksman and their own sense of personal safety.

■

Viktor's room is just down the hall from Jeffery's. Louis's former room, now empty, is between them. Viktor had already been there for some time before Jeffery moved in—Jeffery doesn't know for how long— but Jeffery remembers that his first day at the Burrow, Viktor just stood in the hallway and watched him carry his boxes of books, toiletries, clothes, and his computer through the front doorway and down the hall to his new room, without offering to help. The whole time, nearly an hour, Viktor's huge hands rested at his sides. Jeffery later described them to Raymond as "two slumbering mastiffs."

Still, whenever Jeffery meets Viktor these days in the communal kitchen as Jeffery is putting away groceries someone has left out on the counter—a more regular occurrence than you might guess—Viktor will sometimes pick up a box of cereal or a can of evaporated milk and put it where it's supposed to be. When Viktor says anything at all, it's about his work, some

arcane sentence about the rise or fall of credit somewhere in the world. It's a subject, Jeffery guesses, that
has to do with Viktor's scheme of buying and selling
stock online. Viktor's hair is the color of mud.

The two men take care never to mention Madeline.

■

Louis's room still hasn't been rented, and Jeffery is
not sure why. It has to be despite the cost, which is
extremely low; everybody agrees about that. Maybe,
Jeffery thinks, Louis will be coming back one day, and
it's being saved for him.

The next door to Madeline's room is Heather's.

And Heather? Who is Heather, really?

Well, for one thing, Heather is young and thin with
long, straight blond hair and sort of cute freckles on the
bridge of her nose.

■

## HERE IS A CHART TO MAKE THINGS MORE CLEAR:

| Inside the Burrow | Outside the Burrow |
| --- | --- |
| Jeffery | The Captain |
| Raymond | Louis |
| Madeline | Junior |
| Viktor | |
| Heather | |

■

Lives like sponges: half sponge, half filled with something else.

■

The Captain stands in the living room of his house and stares out the picture window that has been especially modified to remind him of the view from the bridge of the *Valhalla Queen*, minus the icebergs, of course, as he holds a grayish mug filled with hearty seaman's coffee in one hand and a bear claw, just out of the toaster oven, in the other, and gazes out onto his broad front lawn. He does this nearly every morning, but this particular morning he gasps because what does he see but a large hole surrounded by a ring of fresh dirt, as if some enormous gopher arrived from God knows where only to settle in the neighborhood and, specifically, beneath his front lawn. And no sooner does he imagine a gopher of the size it would take to make this hole, than he tries to put it out of his mind. It is a foolish thought, he thinks. But if it isn't a gopher, what could it be? Is he somehow still dreaming?

Still carrying the bear claw, the Captain leaves his coffee mug behind and walks out onto his lawn. (It is curious, he thinks, that after all those years at sea, his lawn has turned out to be what he's most proud of). And then, it is no dream (!), because right in front of him is the hole, eighteen to twenty inches in diameter, which, despite the relatively small amount of dirt that surrounds the opening, appears quite deep. This must mean, he reasons, that it was tunneled from beneath, so that the greater part of the dirt fell downward, back into the hole, where something or someone at the other end must have taken it away.

His appetite gone, the Captain goes back inside. He tosses what's left of the pastry in the trash. The ways of land are still strange to him, and in truth he is not sure how ordinary or how extraordinary it is, from a landsman's perspective, for a person to wake one day and find a giant hole in his front lawn.

Yet, it's not that simple, because this hole reminds him of something—something that has a name, or *had* a name once—but whether out of his own past or some old story, he can't be sure. For a moment he stands motionless, one hand on his marble mantelpiece, the other placed across his forehead, a tableaux: *An Old Sea Dog Trying to Remember,* as meanwhile his memory breaks like low waves upon a distant shore in search of an answer. Break, break, break . . . nothing. Clearly, the waves have insufficient power to erode the shore deeply enough to reveal the answer hidden behind its rocky outcropping. It must be low tide or something.

But the Captain has no time to waste. He has another presentation to give that afternoon, so he calls his gardener and explains the situation as best he can. He tells the man to fill in the hole and cover the top with new turf so it blends into the rest of the lawn. "I'd like the place to look as seamless as the sea itself," he says. "Just make sure that when anyone steps on it, it's perfectly filled in. I don't want any lawsuits from people breaking their legs."

Then he thinks some more. Maybe it wasn't the *hole* whose name he was trying to remember, but the name of whatever once had lived inside, whatever might have crawled out onto his lawn, and from there out into the world.

■

And Heather? What kind of name is that? Heather is kind of a cute name, true, but a spooky chick, Jeffery concludes. Should he try to get something going with her? He can't make up his mind.

■

*Like sponges? Sponges?*

■

*Oh Heather*, Heather thinks, *when you first agreed to live in the Burrow, why, why, why didn't you spend a little more time considering the potential toxic effects of living in conditions of no sunlight plus communal food?*

In other words, Heather is beginning to question the wisdom of her move, because, sure, the Burrow is cheap rent, quiet, and free from all those grabby guys in the last five singles complexes where she could afford only the tiniest of apartments, but, at the same time, it's just so . . . *dank* . . . and, speaking of time, when *was* the last time she got out?

But in her defense (and on the other hand), it sure *is* easy for a person to stay once she's there. It's easy to fall into a routine. Morning arrives: you wake; food appears and you eat it because after all it's coming out of your rent—you paid for it. And even though other people have poured from the milk carton before you (maybe even drunk straight from the carton), and sometimes you wind up getting the bottom part of what's left in the cereal box—broken flakes and all—and if, say, you left a half plate of lasagna in the fridge, then two nights later you have a craving for a little pasta before bedtime, when you go to look for it, there's only a fifty-fifty chance it will be there (so in the end, you wind up helping yourself to somebody else's cold chicken), still, it's not exactly slave conditions.

But . . . *but what?* Because even though all this trading food back and forth doesn't seem right, Heather can't pinpoint what's wrong about it, exactly, and what's very weird is that nobody around here ever complains about the missing chicken or accuses her of taking it, even though she did. *So what's the problem?* Well, nothing, though she does have to admit this place makes her nervous. On the other hand, she must be at least a little happy, otherwise why would she still be here? And did she mention that the rent *is* a bargain? She did. It is. It is a *huge* bargain. Which makes everything that much more confusing.

*Or*—possibly it's worse. Maybe it's not the Burrow at all, but that her job has left some sort of mark on her, a bum's mark, meaning: *Here walks a loser, a person not worthy of your full respect, a person only to be passed by and despised.*

*Or*—on the other hand (are we on the third or fourth hand by now?), she also has to admit that it feels as if her fellow renters—Jeffery and Viktor (not Raymond, thank goodness), but particularly Madeline—are somehow judging her. Does it have to do with her job? She can't remember ever mentioning to anyone what it is, but maybe they've listened at her door, because no one ever seems to have anything better to do with their time anyway, except Viktor.

*A life made mostly of air*, Heather thinks.

■

Viktor remembers that once someone—maybe his mother before he was dropped off at the orphanage, maybe nuns—cut green sticks from a tree, covered them in mud, and then wiped the mud all over his body, from the hair on his head to the soles of his feet. After he was completely covered (except for his eyes), they used the same sticks to smooth the mud out. "Don't move," they—whoever did this—had said, and so he hadn't. He'd waited, watching the boring clouds and boring leaves until the mud had thoroughly dried. Eventually he was left alone, and when he finally moved, a very long time afterward, the mud cracked and fell off and left him dirty.

Why had this been done? To this day, Viktor has no idea. Was this some folk remedy for having been bitten by a swarm of insects? Could he have rolled in a bed of stinging nettles? Was this a treatment for a rash? A punishment? And what happened after? The only thing he can be sure of is that one day there he was, covered in mud and not allowed to move, and then a long time after that he was moving again, as if nothing at all had happened.

Viktor has never spoken about this to anyone. Why would he?

But also—and this is the most secret part—there was something Viktor found deeply satisfying about being covered in mud, about mud in general.

■

And as for Junior: *Is* he a psychopath?

Well, it depends on what you mean by *psychopath*. If by psychopath you mean: a person with a severe personality disorder, especially one that manifests itself through aggressive and antisocial behavior, *and then*, in addition, you can also come up with a satisfactory definition for that nebulous phrase "personality disorder," to say nothing of "severe," you may well be right. But— and speaking only for himself—Junior says he has a hard time when it comes to pinning that "personality disorder" label down. It sounds like a load of crap to him, he says. Just like the word *killer*, because the very same dictionary that came up with that "personality disorder" definition (the *American Heritage Dictionary of the English Language*) defines *killer* as "one that kills," meaning that absolutely everyone—men, women, children, vegetarians (if you include plants), animals, even some plants—is included. Plus, even if you narrow the definition down to "one that kills people," what with wars, and famine, and economic oppression, you still have a group far too large, in any effective way, to eliminate most of the human race. And even then, if you go the extra mile and narrow it further, to "one who takes a human life illegally," that raises, for Junior, at least, one shitload of red flags: For one thing, under *whose* laws? And are those laws just or unjust? And what do you mean by *takes*, exactly?

So really, when we toss around the words *killer*, or *personality disorder*, or even *psychopath*, as people so often casually do, who is it we think we're excluding?

Hardly anyone, it seems to Junior.

■

Heather listens from behind the door to her apartment until she's sure no one is out there. Then, as quiet as a mouse, she opens the door and tiptoes to the shared kitchen of the Burrow to put on a pot of water for tea. *This is no way to live*, she thinks. *If I had a hot plate or even an electric teakettle in my room I wouldn't have to be doing this.* But the rules of the Burrow specifically forbid these appliances because of old wiring or some such. Back when she first arrived she thought about whether she wanted to put up with that rule or not, and at the time it seemed a decent trade-off for the extremely low rent. Now she wonders how anyone would even know. It's not as if they inspect her room or anything like that, at least not that she is aware of.

Whoever *they* are.

Tonight in the kitchen there's a package of arrow-root crackers—her favorite—in a cupboard, and one of the good things about arrowroot crackers is that no one else in the Burrow much eats them because they're so bland, but that's exactly what Heather likes: they're baby food, the kind of thing a mouse would nibble on. They're forgettable, like her. But was she always forgettable? Wasn't there a time when her name, Heather, meant the out-of-doors and springtime and a fresh scent? Yes, indeed.

She remembers the first day of kindergarten, when kindly old Mrs. Charles said to all the other kids—because Heather's mother had forgotten to pack her a lunch until the last minute and as a result Heather was the very last to arrive in class—"Children, I'd like you to meet Heather." And Mrs. Charles had said it with such happiness in her scratchy old voice that it felt as if the old lady teacher had always known Heather but hadn't seen her for a long, long time, and now here she was. It felt to Heather as if Mrs. Charles was blowing a fresh breath straight from the outdoors into every corner of that classroom, a little puff of air that was contained inside her own name, *Heather*, as if she herself were hearing it for the first time. But by the time she got to the sixth grade, her name had worn itself down to Heather-Whatever.

Sometimes Heather dips the arrowroot crackers in tea (she likes Earl Grey) and sometimes she eats them on the side and uses the tea to wash down the crumbs, because, she has to admit, they *are* pretty dry. Tonight she's dipping them, and the hot tea feels good on her throat, which is sore from talking on the phone to maniacs and psychopaths all day.

If only there was someone else she could talk to. There's Raymond, of course—he's strange, true enough, but he also seems kind of sweet in the way that makes a girl feel safe.

■

To the *St. Nils Eagle*

Dear Editors,

I was disappointed last week after reading your account of the Southside Archery and Crossbow competition to find that although the scores for various "traditional" bows were reported in some detail, the crossbow results, either through deliberate omission or simple error, were missing.

Unless you step up the standards of your reporting to include *all* the news, you should know this current subscriber will not remain so indefinitely. Let this be a warning.

Yours Truly,
A Seeker of Truth

■

And then there is also *casi tocándose*: almost touching.

IV

■

*Oh five dropouts came to farm one day*

*To grow some pot and also hay*

*Because the rest of the world was in an uptight way*

*Except for Grandpa Stoner*

    —an excerpt from the theme song to *Mellow Valley*

■

As long as the Captain can remember, there has never been a day in which a part of him was not prepared to die right then and there on the spot, wherever that spot might be, but of course, in varying degrees. For example, on an average day, maybe up to thirty or forty percent of him would be just as happy to call the whole thing—what one of his old first mates, Steig, used to call this "hollow charade"—over and done. In other words: *Good-bye. So long. That's it, friends; I'm out of here.*

On a very good day, the percentage might go down to about five or ten, but on a bad one, it could shoot up to eighty or ninety. Today, just for the record, on his way to the lecture he's supposed to give, he would peg things at about twenty-three—not too bad. He calls this his "Death Quotient," and in the past, whenever he found himself in a tough situation, one where daring and sacrifice were called for, a high Death Quotient gave him an edge.

■

In the first episode of *Mellow Valley*, Mom, Dad, and Junior, their teenage son, find themselves stopped on the edge of a small midwestern town after their VW bus breaks down on their way to attend a rally in Washington, DC, to protest the Vietnam War. The family is dressed in a variety of seventies outfits: Norm, the dad, wears a fringed jacket and puka shell necklace. The mom, Judy, is in a granny dress and headband. The teenager, Junior, is in bell-bottoms and sports a vest covered with peace buttons. Hearing that the repairs to the bus will take a few hours, the family decides to wait in the local diner, where they are intently ignored by the waitress and the rest of the customers. This enrages the usually peaceful Norm, and Judy, exhausted by the stresses of this trip, begins to weep. "This is all a tragic mistake," she tells Junior, who is trying to pretend he does not know his parents. "Do you think there is any chance at all that we were right to intervene in Southeast Asia?"

Finally, a grizzled old farmer, a person who believes in giving everyone a fair shake despite their appearances, stands up and, leaving his booth in the corner, where he's been nursing a cup of coffee, walks to the counter and orders a whole deep-dish apple pie.

"Put it on my tab," he tells the waitress, Ellie. Then he takes the pie back to his booth, where, pulling out a jackknife with a staghorn handle, he divides it into quarters. Next he opens a leather bag on the seat next to him and extracts a dirty block of cheddar, which he slices into four gigantic chunks. After placing a piece of cheese on each slice of pie, he walks over to the table, where Judy, having used up nearly a whole dispenser's worth of napkins on her tears, has finally started to settle down.

"Why don't you all come on over and join me? It seems as if some folks in this here town have done forgot their manners," he says, looking around.

The family is happy to have the pie—the cheese, too. In the course of eating, Norm confides to the man, whose name is Grandpa Stoner, that instead of driving from one futile peace rally to the next, he would much rather find a plot of land and get back to the primal vibrations of the earth. He asks Grandpa Stoner if he knows of any farms in the area that might be available to rent. Grandpa Stoner takes his time thinking about it, finishes off his piece of pie and cheese, and calls for more coffee, which Ellie, shamed by the old man's actions, brings to Norm, Judy, and Junior "on the house."

It's possible, Grandpa Stoner says, if they are serious and they can pass a credit check, that he personally might be willing to rent out his own farm to them. "I'm getting a little too old for sowing and harvesting," he says, "but if you folks care to try it out, I could hang around for a while to show you the ropes. After that, well, we'll just see what happens."

Everyone agrees this is a good idea. The VW bus is fixed and, as they follow Grandpa Stoner's dusty pickup out to his place, Norm spots a pair of hitchhikers trying to get a ride. He pulls off the road and introduces himself. They are a young girl named Heather and a former member of the Special Forces, Sergeant Moody, who is struggling to forget the horrible things he did to various villagers he came into contact with in South Vietnam. The Sergeant asks if, by any chance, they might have room on their farm for an old soldier.

Judy looks at him. "You're not that old," she tells him, "certainly not compared to Grandpa Stoner, and your hair is a lot better than Norm's." She goes on to say that although they haven't seen the farm as yet, it sounds as if they'll have a lot of room, so he's welcome. Heather, who is returning from an unsuccessful audition as an underwear model, asks if there's room for her, too. She explains that she's sick of the shallow values of today's society, and longs for something more spiritual and meaningful than the mindless displays of her breasts and buttocks she's experienced in the past. To the delight of Junior, Norm says yes.

Then follow several comic scenes: Junior attempts to coax a stubborn donkey to go into its stall, Heather tries to milk a cow, and Sergeant Moody, suffering, as it turns out, from PTSD after being shot at by several members of his own platoon, dives under the chicken coop the first time Grandpa Stoner rings the dinner bell, only to emerge covered with white feathers.

And why did Grandpa Stoner think renting out his whole farm to an expanding bunch of strangers was a good idea? He asks this very question in an amusing monologue conducted in the farm's outhouse, where he has gone to rethink his offer, debating the pluses and minuses of the situation while turning the pages of a *Whole Earth Catalog* he found in the back of the VW bus. In the end, just as he's about to tell everyone he's made a huge mistake, Judy walks out of the kitchen with a batch of her famous hash brownies. Later, a hilarious discussion ensues on how to achieve world peace, with suggestions ranging from Sergeant Moody's "to kill anyone who isn't peaceful" to Heather's heartfelt speech that "if we all just love one another, things will work out the way they are meant to."

In the end they decide that while achieving peace for the entire world is a near impossibility, if a person, or a group of people, for that matter, can find peace in his or her own life, that might well serve as a model for the rest of mankind. They decide to call their place (unsurprisingly, because it is the name of the show) "Mellow Valley." Finally Grandpa Stoner declares, "If you five can make it, then maybe anyone can."

■

Mud baths! Yes! Once he was grown Viktor made it a point to visit his local spa at least once a month, sometimes more, for a good mud bath, where, lying enclosed in a garment of sulfur-smelling clay, with only his eyes and lips uncoated, he could imagine that he was invisible, that nobody could see him, and nobody could hurt him, and nobody could make fun of his hands because they were now hidden in mud, pressed against his thighs like the swellings on the trunk of some kind of a tree or another.

Except that—wait!—come to think of it, since he arrived at the Burrow he hasn't had even one mud bath, probably because he's been busy making money hand over fist. Big hand over big fist.

■

In Heather's dream, she's a bird of some sort, but also— you know—Heather, and flying across the country with a big flock of other birds, looking for a place to land, to get a little snack, and rest. Hour after hour they fly, and her arms are getting sore, but because she's at the very back of the flock there's no one she can tell this to, nor does she have any idea where she's headed. *A follower*, she thinks, *that's all I'll ever be*. But whoa! Now everyone ahead of her is dropping down to a place that looks pretty nice. There is water and duckweed and she can see other ducks already there, but just as the leaders are about to land, something goes wrong. The leaders start falling out of the sky! *Pull up, Heather!* she tells herself, and she does, just in time, but her arms are aching even more, and who knows when she'll ever find a place to land?

■

For Madeline, the oddest thing about the Burrow is all the mirrors. Whoever decorated the place—if you could call it decoration—must have thought that in a building without windows, mirrors would make up for the complete lack of any view, or sources of external light, whatsoever. The result being that mirrors are everywhere, not only in the places you'd expect—like the bathrooms, at the ends of halls, and in living rooms, and the one above her bed, of course—but also on the backs of doors and in the kitchen, where there's a big one behind the burners of the stove. It's a special pain to keep clean because of all the grease that splatters on it.

So everything reflects everything else, like living in a fun house, she thinks, but honestly, whether all these mirrors do any good at all is anyone's guess, because while it's true, they *do* reflect the light, they also multiply the dark. Even so, she's mostly used to them by now. That is: Madeline hardly thinks of mirrors at all except when Jeffery, in one of his lame efforts to be funny, pretends the mirrors are two-way, and starts talking to whoever's on the other side.

Ha ha.

■

In the second episode of *Mellow Valley*, the commune's very first crop of marijuana is threatened by the same drought that is also killing the corn, alfalfa, and soybeans on the surrounding farms. "It looks as if your little experiment is going to come to an end as rapidly as it started," Grandpa Stoner tells everyone, in a group meeting he calls after returning from an inspection of the dying plants one dusty afternoon.

And all does seem lost, until the newcomers pool their knowledge in an attempt to find a way to solve their problem. First, Sergeant Moody recalls an obscure method of rice irrigation used by South Vietnamese farmers, many of whom he killed for no reason at all. In places where there wasn't sufficient water to make an actual rice paddy, he said, the wily farmers—no doubt sympathetic to the Viet Cong—used a system of inter-connecting bamboo tubes to carry water to each individual plant. Then Junior sacrifices the tubing on his hookah to make a prototype of the system Sergeant Moody is describing to help them visualize the concept. Norm, with the help of the elderly town librarian, Mrs. Bachhaus, researches which varieties of cannabis use the least amount of water, and Judy, pretending that she is creating a piece of installation art, goes to the local hardware store and orders about a quarter mile of plastic tubing, pumps, and connectors. Working together, the members of the commune rip out most of the dying pot plants, save what few parched leaves they can find, and use them to get high as they wait for the equipment to arrive.

When everything is delivered, Heather, Judy, and Junior plant the new, drought-resistant plants, bought from a fellow peacenik in the dry, southwestern part of the United States, as Grandpa Stoner works alongside Sergeant Moody and Norm to assemble the new irrigation method. "You may be city slickers—no offense, Heather," he says, "but I have to admit there's a half chance that this crazy idea just might work."

The new crop flourishes.

■

So in the way that sometimes very different cities, such as Lima, Ohio, and Lima, Peru, share the same name, we now have two Heathers here. One is the Heather who acted in *Mellow Valley* and the other is a different Heather, who by coincidence has the same name, Heather, but who now lives in the Burrow. And although they are not the same person, it *is* a little confusing because the Heather who is in the Burrow thought she would be an actress one day, that is, that *she* would be the world-famous Heather, and the Heather who acted in *Mellow Valley* would be, well . . . a nobody.

How could she believe this? Well, because of a single moment: After Heather-who-is-in-the-Burrow's memory of that kindergarten specialness (thanks to Mrs. Charles, so her name, Heather = a fresh breeze) more or less evaporated with every ascending grade level, it was a sad and beaten-down Heather who one day walked into Mr. Kaminsky's Theater Arts class in high school. And there, almost as if by magic, the minute she had to introduce herself ("Hello, my name is Heather") she could start to feel that old specialness come back, as if she were important, and she found herself occupying a platform slightly higher than everyone else that she hadn't even known she'd stepped onto.

Acting made her feel like *Heather!* again, and she *was* good, she was better than good, the only problem being that when she was up on the stage with everyone watching her and applauding her, one part of her always knew that people were watching and applauding her not because she *was* Heather, but because she was pretending to be someone else. The point being it was anybody *other* than the real Heather they were applauding; it was a complete stranger they were praising.

And now, waiting behind the door of her room in the Burrow, Heather hears a small noise in the hallway. She holds her breath for a few seconds—not that it makes any real difference—until whoever it is passes by her room and goes back to their own room. If only, she thinks, she could be an actress like the one on *Mellow Valley* who shared her name. She wouldn't be here at all.

■

## IN CASE YOU ARE CONFUSED:

| The Cast of *Mellow Valley* | Residents of the Burrow |
|---|---|
| Norm | Jeffery |
| Judy | Madeline |
| Sergeant Moody | Viktor |
| Heather* | Heather |
| Junior (a psychopath)** | Raymond |
| The Captain*** | |

*Heather, the character on *Mellow Valley*, was actually an actress named Angela Morrison, who, as coincidence would have it, was killed in a car accident at the exact moment the other Heather, the Heather of the Burrow, was saying her name to Mr. Kaminsky, so technically speaking there was a current vacancy in the realm of celebrities with the name of Heather.

**Junior, a member of the cast of *Mellow Valley*, whose character's name, Junior, happens to be the same as his actual one, Junior (Lima, Ohio, et cetera), has become, in the years that followed his appearance on the show, a psychopath with a fascination for crossbows.

***While never an official member of the cast of *Mellow Valley*, the Captain was hired as a consultant for one episode, never aired.

■

*Lives made of nothing but air, without even the layer most sponges have to separate the outer world from the inner one. Or possibly capturing the outer one and making it the inner one. It's hard to explain.*

■

The third episode of *Mellow Valley*, subtitled "The Nature of Hope," is the one in which all the characters on the show suddenly notice that, especially during certain hours of the afternoon, Grandpa Stoner is impossible to find, and when people ask him what he does during those hours, he refuses to answer. Naturally everyone becomes worried, but eventually Junior tracks him down at the local animal shelter. There, it turns out, Grandpa Stoner has been spending a part of every day playing with farm dogs who were left behind by owners who moved away to find work in the city. Sometimes their owners' farms were foreclosed upon, or else their marriages fell apart under the disappointment of one bad harvest after another, or just from the pressures of balloon payments due on their homesteads as a result of taking out bad loans from unscrupulous lenders. At the shelter, Grandpa pets each of these dogs and talks to them, trying to make them feel better about their situation, which, he reassures the animals, is only temporary.

"But Grandpa," Junior says, dismayed, "don't you realize you are just raising the hopes of all these dogs, insofar as all of them—or at least ninety-nine percent of them—are doomed? What good does that do? Don't you think you are only increasing their sense of betrayal at the end, when, expecting a pat and some kind words, instead they are dragged off to be gassed, thus making their last moments even worse than they would have been?"

"Not necessarily," Grandpa Stoner answers. "Dogs can't see into the future any more than you or I, and studies show possibly less. Ergo: we all know we're going to perish in the end. Does that mean we should deny ourselves whatever pleasure we can find along the way? Consider that these animals' hope might last for weeks, or at least days, while this sense of betrayal you speak of will last only a minute. Are you so afraid of dying that you can't see anything else in the room? Please tell me it isn't so, Junior."

Junior doesn't know what room the old man is talking about, let alone what he is supposed to be seeing in it—tables? lamps?—so he waits until everyone has sat down to the dinner table that evening before he returns to the question of pleasure versus truth that Grandpa raised at the shelter, and from that point on the rest of the show becomes more or less a debate along those lines. Grandpa Stoner, Norm, and Judy take the side that momentary distractions are necessary and, in fact, unavoidable. Heather, Junior, and Sergeant Moody—who provides several gruesome examples from prisoners-of-war he held captive for a time, generally a short time— represent the case for unflinching pessimism.

In the end nothing is resolved, but at the time *TV Week* called it "A rare, if unsuccessful, example of a thoughtful situation comedy on a network that has become a byword for the total vapidity of its offerings."

■

## THE TECHNICAL SIDE OF THINGS

Meanwhile, outside the Burrow, in a room in a totally different part of the city, away from the tall buildings and the mom-and-pop grocery stores, far from the sheet-metal fabrication plants, the fabric shops and Internet start-up ventures, in a room lit by bad artificial light, filled with brass gauges, machinery, boilers, tubes, wires, and compressors, and also plenty of cranks, levers, and wheels, two men are working. At the moment, both are awake, but soon one of them will retire to another room, a small room right next to the one they currently share. And in that second room, the man, after removing his heavy boots and taking off what he calls his "funny hat," will take a nap on the single cot.

While he sleeps, his partner, whose own hat remains on, will continue to operate the machinery in the larger of the two rooms.

Their names are not important, but their jobs are very important.

■

And every once in a while—say, every four or five years—some young executive full of self-importance will have the bright idea of releasing all the episodes of *Mellow Valley*, complete with outtakes, as a boxed set. Or he'll even suggest they bundle up what they already have and send them out of the country to people still wearing loincloths and shooting arrows, to places where they are so starved to see anything at all that terrible acting and weird story lines aren't negatives. In other words, he'll say, let's market the show in fourth- or fifth-world places and we can squeeze a couple more bucks out of the old film library. But then he'll sit down and watch the series and understand what a disastrous idea that is. So that will take care of that until the next bright young executive comes along.

■

Are objects in the mirror more distant than they appear? Honestly, Raymond doesn't know, since, despite the tremendous number of polished mirrors in the Burrow, the only time he looks at one is when he has to, which is hardly ever (though he did more often when Madeline was with him, in order to look nice and make her like him). But these days, when he looks at all, it's only to imagine how he would appear to Madeline if she ever changed her mind and wanted him back, which, even to him, is an idea, based on his image in the mirror, that appears increasingly far-fetched.

But in any case, he can't say that *he* himself seems distant, can he?

■

People always believe that words will save them, but they are wrong, Heather thinks. Likewise, all those people who write letters, from prison and elsewhere, from places of entrapment and incarceration, those who believe their words will get them out, are wrong. And also those who sing their words in stupid love songs, or scratch them on trees, or have them carved on tombstones wanting to have "the last word," or print them in newspapers as letters to the editor, and in books; people who think that just because the words are printed they are somehow special, like the guys who call her on the sex line because they think their words have some kind of reality of their own, that because their words are the same as sex to them, then Heather repeating their words back to them must for them be the same as having sex with her, and though Heather *does* concede there may be some overlapping between words and the physical world from time to time—such as when you write words on a Post-it note, and you have the words and you have the Post-it note, which you can stick anywhere you want, moving it around your apartment so you can see it better and help yourself improve who you are—who you *will* be—she cannot convince herself that the neurons firing in those assholes' pinheads when the sex words are said can possibly be identical to the ones firing when actual human contact is being made. Which is a point, come to think of it, that is largely in favor of the sex phone line, because the phone sex neurons are, at best, only in the *neighborhood* of those neurons involved in actual contact—maybe next-door neighbors—and being next door is *not* the same as being in the same house together, eating at the same kitchen table or having sex in the same bed, and sometimes things are better that way.

It's like a dream: if the morning after having a dream a person wants to remember it, she can't look for it in the same place where she keeps her actual stored-away experiences, because no matter how much a person may want to remember a specific dream she once had, even if she had an electrode and pushed a button to stimulate the part of her brain where actual experiences are stored, she wouldn't get any dreams at all, but only get actual experiences. In other words, if a person wants to stimulate a dream, she has to go somewhere else entirely, somewhere next door to her house, though not her house at all. And maybe not even next door, but still down the street or on the next block, though in the same neighborhood—which is her brain, of course—a satisfying thought. So when those high school parents who came to see *Oklahoma!* were applauding "I'm just a girl who can't say no," who was it they were applauding? And why exactly is this an argument in favor of phone sex? She was going somewhere with this, she is sure, but just where eludes her.

Nonetheless, Heather wonders, aren't *all* thoughts like Plato's Cave (a place she imagines looks a lot like the Burrow) in that we are all chained and looking at the shadows cast by the fire on the wall of the cave, believing they are real when they're not? Although come to think of it, didn't Plato say that even if you did somehow manage to unlock your chains and take a stroll outside the cave, once you left the cave you couldn't come back inside again because you would be attacked by all your ex-friends, those cave dwellers, for being crazy because you would be describing things they couldn't understand. In this case, however, Heather can't picture anyone who lives in the Burrow attacking anyone, except possibly Viktor, who strikes her as, well, as having some dark personal issues, and maybe that woman, Madeline. And wasn't "Plato's" also the name of some sex club that opened around the time that *Mellow Valley*, the show that feautured the other Heather actress, was on the air?

So Heather keeps listening to her callers pour their hearts out on the other end of her phone line (her cell phone), and sometimes she hears them use truly bad words accompanied by loud thuds and slippery sounds because they get excited when she says things like, "Wow, you are so big, I want your cock in me," a phrase that Betty, her trainer, told her to say at least twice every conversation if Heather wants to have them coming back, and which phrase Heather now keeps on a Post-it by the phone to remind her to use it, except she wrote down only the initials (WYASBIWYCIM), just in case

a Burrow inspector, as absurd as it sounds, *did* come
into her apartment looking for a hot plate, or electric
teakettle, and saw the initials. That way he would say—
if he said anything at all—something like, "Wow! That
looks Welsh." Or maybe Polish.

Could Raymond be Polish?

■

"Viktor," Jeffery says, "do you think there's a life after
we die?"

"I don't know," Viktor says. "Isn't the important
thing that we get what we want in this one?"

■

In Junior's dream he is at a carnival, a small one, the
kind that travels from neighborhood to neighborhood
throughout the year, with smallish rides—nothing
scary—and lots of small booths, like the ring toss and
throwing baseballs at milk bottles. The booth he is at
now is his favorite: the shooting gallery, the kind where
patrons aim their BB guns at dented metal silhouettes
of ducks that are drawn along by a conveyer belt that's
hidden behind fake waves, painted bright blue, but in

his dream, instead of a BB gun, he's got a crossbow. *Bam*, he hits one, and then *Bam*, another. In his dream he can't miss.

And why *doesn't* someone open up a shooting gallery for crossbows? It could be a big hit, Junior thinks. He'll store that one away for the future.

V

■

For the record, right now the Captain's Death Quotient is roughly forty-five.

Probably because he's thinking about how something as simple as a birthmark in the shape of an anchor can turn your whole life into one big joke.

To say nothing about the deep, invisible hurt that comes with it, the hurt that has no mark on it at all, but is there anyway, because it doesn't seem fair when you know you are so much better than everyone else, objectively speaking. You are so much stronger and more intelligent, but then, any moment you happen to be away from your chauffeured limousine, maybe not wearing your uniform because it's at the cleaners, right at that moment a stray breeze can come by, blow the hair off your forehead, and any complete moron walking by has permission to point at that anchor on your face and laugh.

Even twilight souls.

■

*Polish!* Heather could laugh in this so-called inspector visitor's face about the Polish on her note because if he wanted to take the trouble to find out, one of her clients happens to be Polish—his name is Stan—but as far as she can determine no one has ever been in her room except for her and, of course, whoever lived there before her. And as for the pervs, which is what Heather calls what Betty calls her *customers*, they never want to know anything about Heather as a person either, because, just like those audiences back in the years of her high school plays, it's not Heather they're applauding; it's not the real Heather they want, or even those selected parts of her anatomy she so lovingly describes for them: clit baby, pussy baby, nipple baby. They all want something else, an abstraction, a pure theory, that next-door-neighbor neuron, and like rich cowards who hunt wolves and polar bears from airplanes, all they want is a story to tell themselves, something safe. They want the experience of hunting, but not to meet anything that might fight back.

Or, returning to the next-door-neighbor metaphor, they want the action to take place next door to their own house, not in it, because, frankly, if it *were* in their own house that would mean they were responsible for everything that happened afterward: for putting things back where they used to be, for keeping up with the mortgage payments, cutting the lawn, emptying the gutters, fixing the pipes. And so when they call and Heather picks up the phone, in truth she's just opening the front door of the house they've always fantasized about owning, and for a little while they can pretend they live there, like those people who visit Open Houses on weekends, never intending to buy. So they ring the bell, and when Heather opens the door for them, even over the phone she can feel the heat from the explosion of their fake happiness driving itself straight into the ceiling of her brain vault like exploding popcorn, or Pop-Tarts, or possibly popovers. *Hooray for us—hooray for you and me—we did it, honey*, sometimes the pervs will tell her, but instead, Heather thinks, what they are saying is: *Hooray for me. I got off. I got it on. I got it up. I got down*, and all the crap she hears on the other end of her line—the panting, pleading, whining—doesn't it all come down to WYASBIWYCIM? You bet. Anyway, what kind of a man, she wonders, could possibly imagine that somewhere out in the world might be a woman who, having talked on the phone about nothing but sex for eight or ten hours straight, would still be excited to get his call, still crave more, still be game, a woman who hears his voice and instantly, just by the sound of his voice alone, is able to measure his cock, even though, truth to tell, she might overestimate the size just a teeny bit? *Hey, remember me?* Are you kidding?

Heather can't imagine any woman who could possibly live up to this, unless it's a woman so deep into OCD that she would be incapable of any other action whatsoever, would have to be fed, a bib around her neck to keep the hot gruel, or whatever they are giving her, from spilling onto her chest while she is humping 24/7, after first having been tied down to slow her humping enough for whoever is doing her feeding—attendants maybe—to get enough nourishment in to keep her alive.

Which is a whole other idea, come to think of it: What *about* those people, women in this case, who've had a stroke, or sometimes a brain tumor of the kind that mysteriously activates their libidos (IWYCIM)? Not such a bad idea, truly, to let *them* take calls instead of her. Let them work off some of their hospital bills, maybe even turn a profit, like those rats she's heard about in laboratories that, between experiments, are hooked up to wheels in cages so their running generates enough electricity to pay not only for their own torture but also for an occasional weekend in the country for the torturers.

Heather looks at herself in the mirror above her bed. Not so beautiful as she once had wanted to be. Not so smart as she wanted to be. Not as young. Not as special. Not as sexy. But every bit as tired as she feels.

Maybe if she went to a library she could find a book that would tell her how to make Raymond notice her, but all the man seems to care about is ducks, and maybe Madeline. He's nice to Madeline, she's noticed.

Tomorrow, maybe. Maybe first thing in the morning, before the phone calls start, she'll get out and find a library.

■

And the fact is not only does having a high Death Quotient make killing other people—especially twilight souls—a whole lot easier, but it also makes a person feel less guilty afterward. A lot less guilty. At least in the Captain's opinion.

■

In the fourth episode of *Mellow Valley*, "Junior Falls into a Hole," Junior, preoccupied with passing the state real estate exam in order to become the youngest realtor in the county, takes a mock exam while walking in the woods behind the backyard of an Open House. It's the sort of event he's been attending more or less for practice, but on that particular day he falls into a hole that had been dug by several of the local children as a prank. It is not particularly deep—six or seven feet— but he can't get out because not only has he sprained both his ankles, but the fall has left him seriously disoriented, triggering a near-psychotic moment that may have originated back in the days when Norm, before he got his rage under control through the use of recreational drugs to become the mellow parent-figure he is today, used to punish Junior for the least transgression by burying him up to his neck in the backyard and leaving him there overnight. Nor, back then, did it help Junior's future mental health that his mother would sneak out every two or three hours to bring him his favorite cookies, oatmeal, interrupting any sleep he may otherwise have gotten. (All this was to be revealed in a subsequent episode of the show called "A Day in Therapy," which, though filmed, was never actually aired.)

In the end, Junior is discovered by a wandering group of Boy Scouts engaged in a project that involves clearing the woods of infestations of the notorious death cap mushroom. They find Junior's plight to be humorous and pelt him with acorns and other woodland detritus until they are told to cease by their scoutmaster who, moments earlier, had been off somewhere returning a baby bird to its nest.

■

For some reason Jeffery can't let the thought go: *Life after death*. Well, okay, it's not technically a thought, but is there, or is there not, anything that follows?

*And if there were, of what would it consist?*

Well, what does his present life consist of?

*Not that much, probably.*

And so what would it mean then, to return?

■

A darkness punctuated by a sliver of light is the way that Junior thinks of his life these days. The light being his life, as shitty as it was, before he got the gig on *Mellow Valley*, but then the darkness that followed *that* light was darker than the dark that used to come before. Because before *Mellow Valley* he was nobody, but at least he had a name, but when the television series took his name and gave it to a character, that meant when the character disappeared it took him, Junior, with it. It sucked dry the original unhappy, but still hopeful, Junior, and left him with just the Junior from the show: in other words, a hopeless buffoon, a fool, and a clown. So much for celebrity. And the more Junior tried to explain that he was only pretending to be a helpless fool in his role in the series, the funnier people thought he was, the more a fool. In other words, he had *tried* to explain things, but the world, with the possible exception of his therapist, Tammy, refused to listen. So was it his fault that finally the dam would have to give way and the water would have to come streaming out in a powerful, endless flood? That Junior would be forced to show those people who laughed at him that he wasn't helpless? And then, wouldn't these very same people be the sorry ones?

*The really, really sorry ones.*

*Soon.*

∎

The fact is that the Captain's celebrity doubtless began some years earlier when a group of starving pirates climbed aboard the *Valhalla Queen* by means of crude but ingenious rope ladders to capture and hold as hostages the entire deck shuffleboard contingent. These ancient sportsmen they threatened to kill unless the Captain agreed to their demands: namely, the contents of two premium tables at the ship's buffet. As disgusted as the buffets personally made him, and no matter how much he sympathized with the truly appalling condition of the pirates who, although twilight souls, were after all fellow seamen, the Captain believed that to capitulate would set a bad precedent for fellow captains everywhere.

As a counteroffer, the Captain proposed what he called "a sporting proposition." He told the marauding seamen that they could have all the food on all the tables of *every* buffet, loaded onto their craft by ten of his best crew members, if they were able to beat their hostages, currently wheezing in a Bovril-sweating knot beneath a nearby awning, in a game of shuffleboard. "You talk big," the Captain addressed the pirate chief, "but let's see how tough you are, my friend."

A gauntlet had been hurled and the pirates accepted. After a brief explanation of the rules of the game and a strategy session among the pirate crew, the pirates, superbly conditioned by months at sea in an open boat, proved unnervingly quick learners, pulling to an early lead. And yet, little by little, experience proved itself, and the doddering group of seniors who, in the nearly two weeks of the cruise, had done little else but shuffle their weighted pucks from one end of the court to the other, triumphed by a single point.

The embarrassed pirates climbed back down their ladders of woven rope, and the passengers adjourned to yet another buffet in the dining room. But in no time this story, complete with pictures snapped on cell phones, was sent around the world, the result being that the Captain made a bundle from fish-product and sea-related endorsements.

So the snowball of celebrity rolled on for him, and the more often the Captain gave his opinion on such things as International Law and Maritime Policy, the more he was perceived to be, if not an expert, at least a familiar face.

"What would the Captain say?" became a phrase heard across certain think tanks and boardrooms of the land. In other words, the Captain's ship had finally come in. He retired from the sea, bought a comfortable house in St. Nils, and spent his time gazing out on his lawn. And so, over the past several years, his Death Quotient has stayed, with an occasional run into the twenties, mostly in the low teens.

∎

Next comes the hilarious episode of *Mellow Valley* in which Norm decides to supplement the cash intake of the struggling commune by learning to repair watches in his spare time.

"How hard can it be," he asks Sergeant Moody, who is busy nursing a sick duck back to health, "considering what a small space there is for things to go wrong in?"

So Norm sends away for a mail-order introductory course in horology, complete with a set of tools, and begins to practice on the clocks and watches on the farm, with the predictable result being that soon every clock on the farm is running at a different speed. In a matter of days, no one has the slightest idea of the time, mixing day for night, afternoons for mornings, all of which leads not only to several missed connections but also to the embarrassing scene—still talked about in certain circles—where Judy accidentally bursts in on Grandpa Stoner as he is in the process of deworming one of the commune's two pigs.

Unaware that she is not the only person with no idea of time, Judy takes it personally. "I don't know what's wrong with me these days," Judy apologizes to Grandpa Stoner.

"Well then, if you don't know, you had better find somebody who does," Grandpa Stoner replies, and so Judy decides to take his advice and goes to the town doctor, a befuddled GP named Dr. Whittaker.

But in Dr. Whittaker's office, Judy, who has nothing at all wrong with her besides a simple urinary tract infection, gets her lab work accidentally switched with another patient who has terminal lymphoma. The result is that everyone on the farm, in the belief that Judy is going to die any minute, runs around trying to make her ridiculously comfortable, as meanwhile Judy appears healthier than ever. Nor have they worked out the clock problem, so getting meals to Judy, let alone the right medications at the right time, is nearly impossible.

Finally, just as they have decided to take Judy to hospice in order to get their lives back on schedule without being distracted by the fatal nature of her illness, they discover that the lethal message of the lab work was not meant for Judy at all, but for the town's librarian, Mrs. Bachhaus, who, outside of feeling tired more often of late, hadn't noticed anything at all wrong. Once she does find out, however, she sinks rapidly, so quickly in fact that Grandpa Stoner, who once in the past had a brief fling with the lady, takes to blaming Judy for the whole business. "She was a sweet woman," he tells Judy, "and if you hadn't stolen her results, chances are that she would still be in a loving mood today."

■

And now, on the very evening of the same day that began with his discovery of the giant hole in his lawn, the Captain, wearing his dress uniform and peaked officer's cap, stands before a crowd of roughly two hundred members of the New Prosperity Group (*rich degenerates*, the Captain thinks) in the library auditorium. Suddenly, smack in the middle of that night's story (it's getting hard to keep them straight), the word *Myrmidons* blows into his mind with the force of a gale at sea.

He stops the story he is in the middle of telling to drink a glass of water. *That's it*, the Captain thinks. *Myrmidons* is the very word he's been trying to think of since he first saw the hole in his front lawn. But who were the Myrmidons, anyway? He remembers reading about them in school, possibly in the classics, but which classic was it, and what were they doing in it? Out of the blue he can feel his Death Quotient jerk upward to about twenty-seven or twenty-eight, and why would a little thing like thinking about a Myrmidon cause that to happen? He has no idea.

■

## ADVISORY TO THE TECHNICAL STAFF

Upon receipt of this advisory the revised schedule for the Force of Flow shall be as follows: Between the hours of 1200 to 1700, 3.5; between the hours of 1700 to 2100, 3.1; between the hours of 2100 to 2400, 4.1; between the hours of 2400 to 0002, 4.2; between the hours of 0002 and 0004, 4.8; between the hours of 0004 and 0008, 4.2; between the hours of 0008 to 1200, 4.0, unless during any of these segments obstacles are encountered, in which case the Flow may be increased by a maximum of 10 percent of its Rate at the time the obstacles were first encountered, reminding all operators once again of the importance of close monitoring. Should these measures prove inadequate, the operators will then make a report to the Central Desk and await further orders from same.

Tech #1:    Do you understand any of that?

Tech #2:    As I read it, they want us to keep an eye on the Pressure Plate as usual, but now we are also supposed to apply a different Flow of Force at different times of the day and night.

Tech #1:     Don't we do that already? I thought that's what we were doing. Don't they know it depends on the resistance?

Tech #2:     For some reason or another they seem to be ignoring the resistance completely.

Tech #1:     Well, in my humble opinion, that's the kind of thing that comes from not being in the field. You know what I think?

Tech #2:     No, what do you think?

Tech #1:     I think we should just keep on doing exactly what we've been doing and not change anything. It's worked well enough so far—not perfect—and you never know what's going to happen once you start tinkering with tradition.

Tech #2:     Tinkering, yes, that's more or less the word for it, all right, and I'm with you.

■

The sixth episode of *Mellow Valley* takes a turn toward the serious as, enraged by the commune's refusal to join in a Memorial Day parade to support this country's pointless military incursion into an impoverished foreign country (Vietnam), the local white supremacist neo-Nazi group plans to burn down the main house of the farm where most members of the commune, except for Grandpa Stoner, sleep.

Their plans, however, are thwarted. With a large can of gasoline on the ground next to them, two of the neo-Nazis peer into the house's small living room window, only to discover that Heather (not the Heather who lives in the Burrow, but the other Heather, the semi-successful actress who could be Heather's double except that the TV one is prettier) is not just not asleep, but in full yoga posture, wearing only a bra and panties. Then follows a mind-bending eighteen minutes for both the Nazis and the television audience who witness this ancient Hindu discipline aimed at perfect spiritual insight and tranquility. At its conclusion, the bewitched neo-Nazi duo decides to allow the commune to exist, if only to allow the two of them—and possibly a few friends as well—to sneak back to the window at some future date and learn more about the threefold path of action, knowledge, and devotion that lies at the heart of this increasingly popular and health-oriented practice.

But the surprise revelation of this episode comes at the very end, when it turns out that Heather knew the whole time that the two fascists were there. So it was Heather, and not the intruders, who was in control of this situation, and her nonchalance translated into the words (which the characters of *Mellow Valley* will come to use in later episodes whenever they wish to indicate that something isn't as bad as it seems): "It's only the Nazis at the window." Which is exactly the sort of line that one can tell its creators hoped would become a national catchphrase, something similar to *Make my day*, or *You talking to me?* But, sadly, it became nothing of the sort.

■

Never *sin tocarse*: not touching.

■

His lecture concluded, the limo at last stopped in the driveway of his house, the Captain is relieved to see that his gardener has filled the hole and that the sod he chose to lay across the top is an almost perfect blend with the grass already there. If a person didn't know what he was looking for, that person wouldn't notice anything at all.

It's been a long day, but it's over, and he can feel his Death Quotient slide back down to about twelve.

■

Fresh stalks, pushing their way up through the grasses and the dirt, into the light and the air.

■

The final episode of *Mellow Valley*, called "People, Let's Come Together," is still described by those few who remember the show as something of a Hail Mary pass at an attempt for relevance, and also to entice its ever-shrinking television audience to follow the show's creators in a bold experiment that was meant to herald a whole new sensibility, one whose strategy was to combine gentle humor with an analysis of some of the most profound questions of life in order to make a better world for all of us.

This legendary twenty-six-minute sequence (with time taken out for commercials) contains virtually no action at all, or at least "action" as it is usually spoken of. Instead, it features the entire cast, including neo-Nazis, townsfolk, and fellow farmers, sitting in a large circle, all puffing away on the reefers handed out by members of the commune, as they describe to each other (and to the television audience) what insights about their hitherto unexamined lives—thanks to their mildly psychoactive condition—they have arrived at.

Now considered a precursor to "Reality Television," and rumored to have been filmed using actual drugs, the show has the distinction of being the only network television production ever to have been cut off after the first four minutes and replaced by twenty-two minutes of public service announcements.

■

Anyway, it was only when the Captain was returning from his successful presentation and was just minutes from his house, seated in the limo, that the Myrmidon thing came back into his head. Weren't Myrmidons in the story of the Argonauts? When Jason threw the boar's teeth onto the ground, they popped up, fully armed, each one—God knows why—just looking around for somebody to slay. *Oh, oh, here comes trouble*, he remembers Jason thinking, but then the future husband of Medea took a stone and threw it, hitting one of them. And the Myrmidon he struck, without even stopping to reason where the stone had come from, attacked the Myrmidon standing next to him, and then another Myrmidon rushed in to help the second one, and somebody else rushed to help the first Myrmidon until there was a general free-for-all, which lasted about ten minutes, max, by which time they were all dead. Then after that Jason went on to get the Golden Fleece and marry Medea. The Captain knows how that turned out.

Or so he remembered it. But just before bed that night, when he is back inside his house, he looks up "Myrmidon" on his computer and realizes he was totally wrong. All those dead warriors in the Jason story didn't have a name. They weren't Myrmidons at all. The Myrmidons were from a whole different story. Myrmidons were the fighters who came along with Achilles to help him out in Troy. Myrmidons had nothing at all to do with holes in the ground, though plenty of them died at Troy as well. The ones who sprang from the earth and then died thanks to Jason were nameless.

■

"*Mellow Valley* reruns," the no-longer-young executive leaving for a promotion will tell the younger one who is to take his place. "I wouldn't open that can of worms if I were you."

■

"So when do you think we'll know if Louis is going to come back?" Viktor asks Jeffery. "I was thinking maybe I could take over his room."

VI

■

| DECOYS | DUCKS |
|---|---|
| Look like ducks | Look like ducks |
| Don't eat | Eat |
| Don't fly | Fly |
| Float | Float |
| Can be worth a lot of money | Inexpensive |
| Silent | Very noisy |
| Take hours to make | Relatively easy to make |
| Painted feathers | Actual feathers |
| No feet | Feet |
| Wood | Flesh |
| No hands | No hands |

■

What Madeline said to Viktor the first time she saw him was, "I really like your hands," even though she was secretly thinking that his hands were kind of grotesque and much much too large for an average human being, so maybe the only reason she said it was to make Viktor feel comfortable, him being a newcomer to the Burrow, or to diffuse her own discomfort, like saying, "That's a really great boil on your neck that you've got going." At any rate, she had been dating Raymond back when Viktor arrived and she was starting to get bored again, being long finished with that pretentious ass, Jeffery, and even though Raymond was—still is—sweet, decoys aside, he was a little lacking in—what?—hotness.

Viktor, on the other hand, is Mister Intense, but only, she now knows, in two areas, fucking and making money, and when he finishes fucking, he more or less forgets about her. And even though she knows she could go back to Jeffery (ugh) in a second, or to Raymond, who at least is an artist and, she knows, still has a thing for her, the fact is it would just be too embarrassing, too awful to have to retrace those particular steps. It would make it seem as if she hasn't made any progress at all during her time here in the Burrow.

Obviously, the simple solution is for Madeline to just get out, to meet people, attend a few concerts, join a fan club or two, hit up the singles bars, et cetera. And so she gets dressed up. She puts on some makeup, fixes her hair, looks nice, and tells Viktor, who is hardly paying attention, that she's going to go out to get some fresh air. *There, that wasn't hard*, she thinks. But no sooner does she reach the front door and put her hand on the knob, is about to give it a twist and walk out to a new, or at least newer, life, than it occurs to her to worry about the wind, of all things. If a wind comes up suddenly, it will blow her hair around, move the bushes and knock over trees. And even if it doesn't do that, it will certainly blow around pollen—not good for her allergies—and force the clouds to streak by overhead only to be replaced by other, and of course newer, clouds, none of them keeping the same shape, and so on and so forth, in a terrifying and meaningless progression, and that's just in the short run.

In the long run the leaves will barely have enough time to fall before their trees are back in bud again, full of squawking birds, which will race around, looking for things to make nests out of, and then, when they've finally stuck the nests together and their babies are born, they'll be busy day in and day out stuffing the same regurgitated swill down the babies' throats, and when they're not doing that, they'll be fighting over the same or similar territories, beneath the same or similar sky, next door to the same ocean, with the same or similar dogs barking at one thing or another that's going by, and the same or similar people laughing or crying. Also there will be the same or similar guys who used to ask her out on dates using the same or similar tired pickup lines, the same meant-to-be-winning gestures, who took her out to the same or similar overspiced or underspiced meals ("Our special today is beef brochette") in those same quaint cafés and similarly hip restaurants—the food not even close to being as good as the stuff that she makes—and then, when the guy, one guy or another, had *sometimes* paid the check at the end of the meal, him asking, as if this were an entirely new concept that had just then occurred to him, "So, what are you doing the rest of the night?" It reminds her of when she used to stand next to one of those automated traffic lights while waiting for it to change while it kept saying "Don't walk," out loud, as if she hadn't heard it a million times already. She hates it when she starts thinking like this.

And then there is also the same or similar fucking, and the unfucking, and the planning-the-rest-of-our-lives-together sessions late into the night, and after them the breakups, and next analyzing the breakups, and starting over. And true, at first it was all sort of okay, all kind of a novelty, too, but now, with her hand on the knob, about to leave the Burrow, it suddenly occurs to her to ask: Are things *that* bad down here? Why go out when you know how it's going to end anyway, which is exactly the same as it's ending here? And the difference between her old life and this one, if she cares to measure it? Well, Madeline thinks, not much, with the advantage to the Burrow being that it is mostly quiet, mostly safe, smoke free, incredibly inexpensive, and mostly illusion free. And Viktor, when he remembers her, is actually decent in the sack.

So she takes her hand off the knob for the moment, goes back to her room, hangs that dress back up in the closet, and heads to the kitchen, where at least she'll be able to whip up some new snack or another, depending on what's in stock.

Maybe she should start small. That night, waiting for Viktor to leave the computer and join her between the sheets, she asks him, "If you were going to sign up for a fan club, whose would you pick?"

■

*The better to touch you with*, is what Viktor tells Madeline, but even so, he'd rather have a pair of normal hands. "You should play basketball with those palookas of yours," the basketball coach had told him back when he was a kid, and so he did, Number 37, but the truth was that he was still short, so things evened out; he could hold the ball like a champ, but he never got a chance to shoot it because his opponents towered over him, and the only thing he got out of the experience was a new nickname—Los Manos.

"Ha, ha, Los Manos," Viktor replied the first time someone called him that. "That's funny." And the following night he made sure to slash the tires of the bicycle of the kid who said it. But by then, *Los Manos* had stuck.

Not that anybody here in the Burrow ever calls him anything but his own name, Viktor, spelled with that *K*, and why it is a *K*, he does not know. Somebody, maybe a nun, once told him that his father-in-absentia was Scandinavian, or German, and possibly a sea captain, though how she would come to have this information he has no idea, so there's plenty of room for doubt.

As a place to live the Burrow is okay enough—a guy can make a lot of money if he wants to, and Viktor does. In part it's because the rent is cheap, but also it's because there are no distractions other than Madeline, which, frankly, leaves plenty of time for a go-getting person to invest online. So he has to say that being here is good, and Madeline is a bonus, because even though when he first arrived she was with Raymond, anybody with eyes could see that she was too much for him to handle. Anyway Viktor knows her type: treat them bad, and they'll come back for more, is his motto. Besides, the first time he ever saw the inside of Raymond's apartment, which is basically wall-to-wall ducks for Christ's sake, he knew it was only a matter of time before Madeline would be running screaming out of there. To him.

Plus, soon, if he can pull it off, he'll have a larger room—Louis's old one—so Madeline can live with him there if she wants to, and give him the money she saves in rent to invest for her. Is she that practical? He has his doubts. For example, just the other day she asked him what kind of fan club he would join, of all things. He told her, "I don't know. Maybe one for that old Captain you see on TV selling fish."

■

And what does Heather do when she is not servicing (an unfortunate choice of words, but there you have it) her clients in the sex trade? Well, oddly enough, she's writing a book. It's for children and it's called *Ballerina Mouse*, about a mouse who, more than anything else in the world, wants to be a ballerina, and this little mouse really, really tries, she does. She practices day and night, hardly taking any time to eat or sleep, but the bad thing is that one of her hind feet—feet being the most important thing to a good ballerina—is deformed, twisted around so badly that Ballerina Mouse can barely walk, let alone jeté or entrechat. So the sad part, the genuinely fucked-up part (and Heather is sorry to use such a word as "fucked-up," but her work vocabulary keeps intruding into the rest of her life, which is why she needs to quit this job) is that Ballerina Mouse will never, ever, be the dancer she wants to be, no matter how hard she tries. And of course, everybody who meets her knows this instantly, but none of them can bring themselves to speak the truth.

And it's exactly because this, or something similar, happens to a lot of people that Heather thinks it would be a good thing for children to read about while they are still young—so they can get used to disappointment—because, truly, hardly anyone gets to be what he or she wants to be. They also should learn that sometimes people lie.

*So how's the writing coming?*

Well, it's practically writing itself, she thinks, except for the ending, which she's having a hard time with because of what she needs to do, which is to make sure the kids 1) don't miss the message that life is kind of disappointing, but 2) still make the ending happy enough that those kids who finish won't slit their tiny wrists, and that's the hard part. Nonetheless, she's getting close; she's sure of it, and then, when she finds just the right conclusion, maybe she'll get lucky and sell *Ballerina Mouse* for a lot of money, and become a famous author, or at least a famous children's author. Then she'll be able to give up this phone sex business, unless, for some reason, she starts to miss it, which she honestly does not think will happen. Though if it does, then she'll only do it when she feels like it.

■

Not that Viktor has anything against Raymond personally. Sometimes, true, when Raymond passes him in the hall Viktor will let out a little quack, but it's just a small one and it's only a joke, and most of the time Raymond will even quack back at him, like it's their private language. Duck Man may be (well, he *is*) screwed up, Viktor thinks, but he's basically all right. At least he's got a sense of humor. And Viktor doesn't begrudge Raymond his former fling with

Madeline at all. If something's being offered to you, why not take it?

He does.

■

In Raymond's dream, Madeline and Viktor are dressed in black and seated on two giant chairs made out of gray concrete blocks stacked (without mortar) one on top of another. Though there are red pillows on the seats, the chairs don't look very comfortable and when, in his dream, Raymond enters the room, Madeline and Viktor remain seated, but raise their arms in the same gesture made by aliens in old sci-fi movies to acknowledge the presence of an earthling. Something like, "Hail, Earthling," or "Welcome to Thoz."

Then Madeline nods once, as if she's saying that Raymond should approach the matching thrones, but at the same moment Viktor shakes his head, as if he's saying, "Raymond, don't listen to her. You stay right where you are and don't move."

So should Raymond approach or not? It's a hard question, and for the rest of the night he just lies in bed, tossing, looking at the dark spectral shapes of ducks along his wall, trying to make up his mind.

■

Tammy, Junior's therapist, fingers her ankh-shaped pendant as she speaks in what Junior regards as her low, sexy voice. "It's been a long, hard process for you, Junior, but I think the worst of it is over."

Junior likes Tammy. She's positive thinking, for one thing, and pretty, for another. She has short brown hair and wears flower-patterned skirts that show off her legs. She smells good, too—something like vanilla mixed with fresh-cut grass, and when he comes in for a session the first thing she does is make him a cup of chamomile tea—to calm him down, she says. Only after he's had a couple of sips will she let him talk.

Because it *has* been one motherfucking hard journey for Junior ever since *Mellow Valley* went down in flames and he went from being a star (well, a *rising* star) right back to being nothing at all, as some (many) people had said he was in the first place. True, he was only a kid when he did the show, but needless to say that just made it worse because he didn't have any examples of what things were supposed to be like, information that kids who have fathers would be taught. So instead of knowing that life is all about disappointments and overcoming them, Junior thought the good times would keep going on even though, come to think of it, *Mellow Valley* wasn't all that good of a time. In many ways, in fact, it was a nightmare. So by this point in his therapy Junior has told Tammy everything: how he hates his stupid name left to him by his Scandinavian sea captain father, the foster homes, and then the series of arrests and being *institutionalized*, as Tammy calls it, at least four times. But now he's out (obviously) and with a little help from the government, Junior lives quietly in his furnished room with not much else besides the stuff the place came with—only a few books, paperbacks, a change or two of clothing, a hot plate, a plate, a sink to rinse his plate, and Old Stag Killer.

"I probably shouldn't be saying this, but I think you are on the road to health at last," Tammy tells him, giving him a tiny hug in the form of her two small hands, grasping each of his upper arms and giving them a single squeeze. "Just keep taking your medication and remember to keep active. What was that sport you said you were doing . . . archery?"

■

It's afternoon in the Burrow, and Madeline and Viktor are lying around his apartment. They have just finished making love and Viktor, unusually for him, is taking a break from the stock market. What the hell, Viktor figures, he may as well ask. "What was it about Raymond?" he says. "What did you ever see in him?"

Madeline looks at him for a minute—a long one. "Oh," she says, "Raymond has his ways." And suddenly Viktor is sorry he asked.

■

"Do you hear that noise?" Jeffery says to Heather as they pass in the hall late one night. Heather looks a little jumpy, as usual, but Jeffery thinks maybe it might be a good time to start a conversation, maybe get to know her better.

"What noise?" asks Heather.

"I don't know. A grinding sound, maybe. It's not that loud, but I can hear it."

"No," Heather says, "I haven't heard it, but then for my job I'm on the phone quite a bit, so I might not notice."

"What kind of job do you have?" asks Jeffery.

"Oh," she says, "just a job." And she darts back inside her apartment, quiet as a mouse.

■

Madeline has left Viktor's apartment to go back to her own, while Viktor is just getting angrier.

*The Duck Man has his ways. What kind of crap is that? Who does she think she is? Doesn't she know who I am?*

He should just pick up and leave, but on the other hand, if he stays in this stupid apartment building, he'll keep making money, and it will be he, Viktor, who will have the last laugh. So far, he figures, since he came to the Burrow and started buying and selling stocks on-line, his investments have averaged about ten percent per month, a rate most professionals would envy, and in fact, it's the very solitude of the Burrow that makes such a return possible. Down here there are no distractions as there surely are for his competitors—those stockbrokers on Wall Street busy with their champagne breakfasts, three-martini lunches, their coked-out weekends, their fashion shows in the Hamptons and gambling trips to Vegas, or maybe Atlantic City. In the Burrow there's nothing at all—unless he counts Madeline—to interfere with his fearsome concentration on making money. *Duck Man*—he has to laugh. How much can he be getting for those pathetic wooden ducks of his? Not much, Viktor thinks, as, meanwhile, his own earnings continue to spiral upward, and then, when he factors in the impossibly cheap rent at the Burrow and the virtually free meals, this place is too good a deal to pass up.

He takes out a piece of paper and a pen and starts to write. His first investment was something like $2,662.00, and he made ten percent right from the start.

That means something like this:

**Month 1:**   $2662 X .10 = 226
**Month 2:**   $2662 + 226 = 2888 X .10 = 288
**Month 3:**   $2888 + 288 = 3176 X .10 = 317
**Month 4:**   $3176 + 317 = 3493 X .10 = 349
**Month 5:**   $3493 + 349 = 3842 X .10 = 384
**Month 6:**   $3842 + 384 = 4226 X .10 = 422
**Month 7:**   $4226 + 422 = 4648 X .10 = 464
**Month 8:**   $4648 + 464 = 5112 X .10 = 511
**Month 9:**   $5112 + 511 = 5623 X .10 = 562
**Month 10:**  $5623 + 562 = 6185 X .10 = 618
**Month 11:**  $6185 + 618 = 6803 X .10 = 680
**Month 12:**  $6803 + 680 = 7483 X .10 = 748
**Month 13:**  $7483 + 748 = 8231 X .10 = 823
**Month 14:**  $8231 + 823 = 9054 X .10 = 905
**Month 15:**  $9054 + 905 = 9959 X .10 = 995
**Month 16:**  $9959 + 995 = 10954 X .10 = 1095
**Month 17:**  $10954 + 1095 = 12049 X .10 = 1204

**Month 18:**  $12049 + 1204 = 13253 X .10 = 1325

**Month 19:**  $13253 + 1325 = 14578 X .10 = 1457

**Month 20:**  $14578 + 1457 = 16035 X. 10 = 1603

**Month 21:**  $16035 + 1603 = 17638 X .10 = 1763

**Month 22:**  $17638 + 1763 = 19401 X .10 = 1940

**Month 23:**  $19401 + 1940 = 21341 X .10 = 2134

**Month 24:**  $21341 + 2134 = 23475 X .10 = 2347

**Month 25:**  $23475 + 2347 = 25822 X .10 = 2582

**Month 26:**  $25822 + 2582 = 28404 X .10 = 2840

**Month 27:**  $28404 + 2840 = 31244 X .10 = 3124

**Month 28:**  $31244 + 3124 = 34368 X .10 = 3436

**Month 29:**  $34368 + 3436 = 37804 X .10 = 3780

**Month 30:**  $37804 + 3780 = 41584 X .10 = 4158

**Month 31:**  $41584 + 4158 = 45742 X .10 = 4572

**Month 32:**  $45742 + 4572 = 50314 X .10 = 5031

**Month 33:**  $50314 + 5031 = 55345 X .10 = 5534

**Month 34:**  $55314 + 5531 = 60879 X .10 = 6087

**Month 35:**  $60879 + 6087 = 66966 X .10 = 6696

**Month 36:**  $66966 + 6696 = $73662

Viktor's favorite months are Month 8, when the interest begins to move forward for the first time at amounts greater than five hundred dollars; Month 23, when he breaks the two-thousand-dollar-per-month mark; and also Month 34, when the total moves from the fifties to the sixties, and at the same time his monthly profits move from five thousand a month to six thousand.

In any case, he calculates that three years from whenever it was he started, he'll have enough to leave the Burrow for good, and maybe rent an office in a skyscraper where, in addition to the ever-increasing profits from his own investments, he can also offer to invest the money of others, taking a small percentage of the return he obtains for them to reward himself. Then, he thinks, the money will start to roll in big time, and if Madeline wants to go back to the Duck Man at that point, well, she's welcome. Even if she wants to stay in the Burrow, Viktor's sure he'll have no trouble finding some other woman who will be happy enough to live with a person who, although he may not have Raymond's *ways*—whatever those are supposed to be—just happens to be rolling in wealth. There's Heather, for one, he thinks. There's something about Heather that Viktor finds interesting, though a little standoffish. He can't put his finger on what it is, but there's something going on beneath that demure surface, and if people care to place a bet to see who the real winner is here—Viktor or the Duck Man—he'll cover that bet. Speaking for himself, Viktor has no doubt at all who will come out on top. Mano a mano, so to speak.

And now it's time to get back to work.

■

Sometimes Raymond wonders what it is like to be a duck: What is it like to have a facial expression so frozen that no one, not even another duck, can tell if you are in pain?

It must be safe in one way, but then sooner or later the hunters come along and say to each other: "Hey, look at those birds out there, bobbing on the pond. We can shoot them because they can't feel emotion."

*But that's not true*, Raymond thinks. *Not even a little bit.*

■

Meanwhile, fresh shoots push up out of the ground like dead fingers. Step down on them, hard, lest they take hold.

■

Who is it that says the following:

"Junior, you put that chair down right now."

"Now leave that two-by-four right where you found it."

"Put down that iron bar immediately."
"Put that cinder block down."
"Put down that crossbow and leave."
*Why, many different people.*

■

*Crossbow?*

■

Madeline and Viktor are in the kitchen one night. Madeline is making a bowl of cinnamon toast and milk for both of them and using not granulated sugar, but the natural unbleached and coarse-ground variety, which someone was kind enough to leave the other day, when Jeffery enters.

"Jeffery," Madeline says, "would you like me to make a cinnamon toast for you? It's not any trouble."

Jeffery weighs the question. It's late, and he's planning to go to bed at any minute. Come to think of it, he's not even sure what made him walk out of his room to the kitchen in the first place. Maybe he's getting cabin fever. "No thanks. But actually, seeing the two of you here like this gives me an idea."

Viktor looks at Jeffery as if for a moment he has materialized from outer space. Why would Madeline be offering to make him toast? Did Jeffery have his ways as well?

"So it's like this," Jeffery says. "Here we are all together in the Burrow and yet how often do we have a chance to sit down and talk? Not often, right? I mean we *do* have the chances, and a lot of them, but we never do it. What do you say we make a point of all of us getting together once a week, here in the kitchen, and we can have a meeting where we can discuss the ideas of the day, and how everybody is feeling, and other various concepts that might occur to us, you know—like life after death, and things like that? That is, if we all agree to do it. Or we could even have an agenda, so after we've finished one subject, at the end of the meeting we could vote on another one to talk about the next week, which would give us a whole week to prepare our thoughts and the like. Or, for that matter, we could do it in rotation, where people choose their own topics, and then when we've finished with those everyone chooses again."

The toaster oven pings, and Madeline puts a couple of slices of hot toast into bowls and pours on a little warm milk. She gives one to Viktor and keeps the other for herself.

"So what do you think," she asks Jeffery, "is Louis ever coming back?"

■

Strictly speaking, the ducks Raymond keeps in his room are not actual decoys at all, but only duck interpretations, or duck tributes, carved from wood, because it's not the act of carving them that makes them decoys; it's the humans who place them where they might attract ducks and lure them for a landing. You could do that with handkerchiefs, or painted rocks, for that matter, and people have done it with those, too. Decoys don't kill ducks, Raymond thinks, people kill ducks, and Raymond would *never* kill anything.

■

Also, Raymond thinks, the reflection of a person in a mirror can never be the same as the actual person being reflected, because the speed of light has to be taken into consideration. No matter how close you stand in front of the mirror, it still takes just a tiny moment to go from there and back again. Everything takes time. Raymond knows this, and tells himself to be patient.

Something big is going to happen soon. He's sure of it.

■

Exits are important. And just because the exit from the Burrow happens to be the same as the entrance, doesn't mean it's any less special: a door leading to a concrete walk that is cracked in a few places, and runs from the street to the front door. The grass on either side of it is tall, ankle high, full of dandelions and burdock, and even a few stalks of bamboo, which, come to think of it, is just another kind of grass. Nobody seems to know whose job it is to keep it cut.

Embedded into one part of the walk, near the street, is a series of bicycle tire tracks that must have been made by some kid years ago, a kid who had been passing by after the cement had been poured, before it hardened. So the kid ran right over it, and maybe the workmen had gone home for the day, or maybe their backs were turned, or they were around a corner, sitting in the shade, having lunch, sandwiches and coffee poured from metal thermoses, swapping stories, exchanging complaints, and didn't see him. How old is that kid now? Does he have kids of his own? Is he still alive? Does he even remember that day?

Near the exit a weed of some unknown variety is poking up, but nobody knows its name.

■

And not just light, but the electric impulses traveling along neural tracks take time as well. So it *always* has to be the case, Raymond thinks, that, like the heads of those guillotined aristocrats back in the days of the French Revolution, we are always dead a micromillisecond before we realize it.

And by then of course it's too late.

VII

■

*How fucked up can one person be? Don't answer that*, thinks Junior, having, for one thing, spent his entire adult life monikered with that stupid kid-name, Junior, and not even a real kid-name, like Rusty or Chuck, but one laid on him by his stupid in-absentia dad, who only stayed around long enough to knock Junior's mom up and then leave him with a name that is a constant reminder of his presence. Junior to what? To whom? As if he could ever find a Senior.

For God's sake, Junior thinks, people take more care in picking out the names of their pet dogs or cats. Especially cats, whose owners seem to get some special thrill from bestowing a name that announces to the world how clever they, the owners, are: Cleopetra, or Drepuss, or Picatso, or Mister Snuggles. But even dogs get better names than he did: Pal, or Duke, or Brutus, or Mauler—names with something substantial about them. *He* could be a Mauler, for example. But *Junior*?

What is Junior if not someone who is young, a person who will be forever second, will remain a permanent child, or, at best, a permanent young adult, a father's heavy thumb atop him?

There has got to be a way to even things out.

■

Sometimes, late at night, Raymond shuts his eyes and pictures Madeline's pubic hair, shy and silent as the red cellophane grass in the basket his mother would leave on the breakfast table on Easter mornings. Sure, there were chocolate bunnies, and colored eggs, and marshmallow ones, but it was that grass he liked the very best, shiny and fragile and mysterious all at once.

*Oh, Madeline*, he thinks.

*Come back.*

Also: *Is there such a thing as an Easter duck?*

Of course there is.

He had one once, a duckling, and it died.

■

It is late at night in the Burrow, and Madeline and Viktor lie awake listening to the sounds of grinding from outside, from deep beneath the earth. They notice that the sounds are getting louder, though not so loud they are unbearable, or anything even close to that. Unable to sleep, Madeline is trying to decide whether or not to go back to her own room and her own bed, but along the way she finds herself returning to a question that's been on her mind for a while. Namely, this fan club business—she wonders whether she should get a leg up on becoming a celebrity herself by first joining a celebrity entourage, to see how the whole business works.

"It seems to me it's a two-part problem," she tells Viktor, who is just starting to doze. "The first part is simply whether to join or not to join. But then," she continues, "assuming the answer to the first part is in the affirmative, the second question to ask is which entourage a person should join, because, predictably, as the number of celebrities grows, so do the number of possible entourages. Should a person become an early adopter, or wait to be sure the celebrity of their choice has real staying power?"

Viktor grunts.

"Here's how I see it," Madeline continues. "Regarding the first part, the part about whether to join or not, the obvious advantage of joining an entourage is that a person who is in an entourage always has somewhere to go and something to do, some personal appearance or new release to look forward to—some behavior of their celebrity to either praise or defend—at least as long as the celebrity is alive. And then, even after the celebrity dies, a person in an entourage can visit their particular celebrity's grave, leave flowers, attend memorials, and collect souvenirs of their celebrity with other members of the entourage.

"But on the other hand," she adds, "this has to be only a short-term solution, because, unless the celebrity one chooses is a megacelebrity, sooner or later the members of his or her entourage will drift away, siphoned off by the entourages of other, more popular and more alive celebrities."

Viktor gets out of bed and walks over to his computer screen, where he studies rows of numbers. London, Tokyo, Berlin. Not much seems to be happening, moneywise. He says, "Is that grinding noise getting louder or is it only my imagination?"

Madeline listens to the grinding some more, happy that, for once, she and Viktor are on the same page.

■

Burrow: an underground passageway, enclosed except for openings for ingress and egress, usually one at either end. Often made by an animal.

From the Middle English *borow*, earlier *burh*, apparently gradational variant of late Middle English *beri* burrow, variant of earlier *berg* refuge, Old English *gebeorg*, derivative of *beorgan* to protect; akin to Old English *burgen* grave, i.e., place of protection for a body; see bury.

∎

Viktor says, "So why do you have to decide this tonight?"

Madeline says, "The reason it is so important to make a decision is that you and I are running out of time, and any day now the world will be divided into three kinds of people: 1) celebrities; 2) those who are in an entourage; and 3) those who aren't. And when that happens, you better believe I want to be either a celebrity who has her own entourage or at the very least a member of an entourage that is important and powerful."

"But isn't the world already divided into people who are in entourages and those who aren't?" Viktor asks, and he thinks he must have struck a note of some kind because Madeline's response is to jump straight out of bed without a stitch of clothing on and stand next to Viktor at his computer, her fluffy pubic hair glistening in the light of the screen.

"Viktor," Madeline says, "you don't understand. I said: Time is running out for both of us. We have to choose. We have to take a leap."

Viktor opens one of his large hands and stares at the lines in his palm as if they are a massive artwork bulldozed into the desert floor. What he's thinking she can't tell. "Maybe, or maybe not," he answers.

■

Raymond is in the kitchen, staring at the bowl full of Grape-Nuts and milk in front of him, as Jeffery rummages around in the refrigerator, mumbling something about having left a beer inside. Suddenly Jeffery closes the refrigerator door and joins Raymond at the table. Even though Jeffery is his best friend, there is something about him that Raymond doesn't quite trust, though it might just be that Jeffery was with Madeline before him, and he can't help wondering if Jeffery, too, is trying to get her back.

"Raymond," Jeffery says, "do you remember that dream you told me about where you were a duck?"

"Yes," Raymond says.

"Well, just suppose," Jeffery says, "that you were a duck in a former life. Do you think that's a possibility?

"A possibility," says Raymond. "Yes, I suppose so."

"Then," Jeffery says, "maybe there's a part of you that carried over to this life. Maybe that's why you like making those decoys so much. And that although 99.9 percent of your former life is gone, there's still a trace that remains, like your shadow on the wall of a building across the street."

"Across what street?" Raymond asks.

"Any street. The street's not important."

"But if there are buildings on both sides of the street and the sun is at one end, how is your shadow going to hit the building?"

"Listen," Jeffery says. "It's late in the day, and the sun is almost down and your shadow is stretching clear across the street and, if you have to know, there are only buildings on one side of this street. You are on the other side."

"So what do you think your former life was?" Raymond asks.

"I'm not sure," Jeffery says, "but I think I must have been highly successful, because I can almost taste it. For sure, though, I wasn't an animal. No offense, but I just can't see myself as a duck or a cat or a mouse."

■

Ballerina Mouse regards her twisted foot. Being a rational creature, she understands that she'll never be a ballerina—so why try? Instead, she uses her time to build a career as a telephone counselor on a suicide hotline and collects little porcelain statues of ballerinas, thus giving her the nickname "Ballerina Mouse" among the many friends she has made, and when she dies all these statues are heaped inside her coffin and buried along with her to keep her company in the next life.

*Heather doesn't think so.*

■

Raymond remembers that in the dream he had where Madeline and Viktor were sitting on their giant thrones, Viktor's hands seemed even larger than usual, so that they weren't like hands at all, but more like two trash-can lids onto which someone had attached fingers.

Possibly, however, that was just due to the visual perspective that came from Raymond's observing Viktor while Raymond was standing and Viktor was sitting down.

■

The truth is that Junior has no idea what his father looks like, except when he looks in the mirror: a tallish individual, not getting any younger, who favors plaid shirts, and who has a beard that makes him look like a lumberjack or a sea captain.

And sometimes, standing in front of the mirror looking at himself impersonating his father, he likes to pretend that his father is talking:

"Junior, how can you be so stupid?"

"Junior, what is wrong with you?"

"Junior, what the hell *are* you thinking of with that crossbow? Aren't you man enough to shoot a gun?"

"Answer me, Junior. What is wrong with you, anyway?"

"Fuck you, Dad," says Junior.

■

Today's lecture is one the Captain has given plenty of times, and it's always a hit, but then, you never know, so he looks around. The hall, a Masonic one, with dark wood and plenty of protractor symbols, is almost full. The hoodlums who have plagued such events at times in the past appear to be absent. So far everything looks good.

The Captain is wearing his dress uniform, of course, complete with peaked hat, fresh pressed trousers, an acanthus in his lapel, and then—*here we go again*—some skinny guy comes up to give the introduction: "fighting pirates to a standstill . . . international authority in matters of the sea . . . colorful . . . beloved spokesperson for seafood jerky . . . etc." He's heard it so many times he's almost nodding off.

Applause, and the Captain ascends the three steps to the lectern. Takes a deep breath. Go. Stands up straight and sort of squints, as if he is looking out through the mist from the wheelhouse, a look he practices some mornings through his front window. "It was a rainy morning in the Nicolas Islands, and I was at a little backwater port called Misha, south of Burma on the Andaman Sea," he begins. He has a nice, deep voice; he always has.

The audience settles in. He can feel them relax. "The sky that day was as black as a . . . and here he pauses not just for dramatic effect, but because he's going to try out a new simile, and wants to get it right ". . . a black bear that has just wandered into a subtropical river and now has emerged to stand dripping over a native, who, weary from a long day's toil, lies taking a nap on his straw mat on the riverbank, unaware that this nap will be his last." *Does that work or does it go too far?*

A few audience members shift in their seats; a couple pokes each other. The Captain is pleased. The truth is, he has only about six talks to draw on, total, but he figures that if he can keep changing up the similes and so forth, maybe people won't notice. Still, sooner or later of course they will, and he'll be out of a living. For now, however, the Captain remains what he is—a minor celebrity—and his talks have become a sort of St. Nils tradition, like the reading of "A Christmas Carol" at Christmas.

The Captain again looks out over the hall. Are the crowds getting smaller? He counts the empty chairs. Fifteen. It's hard to say.

■

Raymond looks at the rows of ducks around him: *At first we humans were animals just like you*, he says to them. *Then things started to change, until what have we become? What are we now?*

The ducks remain silent, and they do not move at all.

■

## TRANSCRIPT OF CONVERSATION FROM
## THE TECHNICAL STAFF

**Tech #1:** What is the name of this stuff they feed us, anyway?

**Tech #2:** They don't have a name for it, but I call it slop.

**Tech #1:** Then why don't *they* call it slop?

**Tech #2:** Are you kidding? Who would eat anything called slop?

**Tech #1:** But you eat it, don't you? I do, too.

**Tech #2:** Well, slop is what I call it when I'm talking about it with you, but the truth is that I made up another name for it, one I don't tell anyone else, but which helps me keep it down.

**Tech #1:** Will you tell me, so maybe I can feel better about eating it?

**Tech #2:** I'm sorry. You'll have to get your own names for things.

**Tech #1:** And why do they get real food, while we're the ones who have to eat this?

**Tech #2:** Honestly, I don't have the answer to that.

I've wondered myself. All I can say is the
reason must be above my pay grade.

**Tech #1:**      You mean *our* pay grade.

∎

Twilight souls, caught somewhere between dark and
light, knowing and unknowing.

    Neither one thing nor another. A crossbreed race.

∎

A cross *bow*.

    And not a race at all.

# VIII

■

At the Masonic Hall, the Captain studies the crowd again; they are still good; they are still with him. He goes on: "I was standing in the shabby office of the harbormaster, a cunning fellow by the name of Ali Khan, waiting to complete the paperwork required before my vessel, the *Shanghai Pearl*, could leave the harbor. The papers were an important matter because, as I stood peering around in the darkness of the man's office, the *Pearl* was still at dockside, loaded with several tons of tuna kept cool on ice. But as dark and damp as it was inside the office, it was still unbearably hot, and the ice aboard my ship was melting fast."

What is it about stories, the Captain wonders, that people want so much to hear them? Is it that they represent a knowledge people imagine they don't have? That stories take people on voyages to places that are different from their own pathetic wanderings? Is it that stories, unlike most people's miserable existences, have definable boundaries, have beginnings and known endings, whereas in real life we discover ourselves dropped onstage midway through some ongoing dramatic series, or maybe a situation comedy, and we're expected to figure out what role we're to play, never knowing if this current episode will be the last or will be renewed by the network for another season? Sitcoms—he knows a little something about them, too, he's sorry to report.

"I could see Ali Khan sipping some native firewater from a tall bottle on his desk," the Captain continues, "as he measured me in the light of the two oil lamps burning in his office. The lamp on his desk cast its yellow glow over his official papers, while the second lamp, on top of a file cabinet, had been seemingly placed for the sole purpose of illuminating Old Lucifer, a stuffed fighting gamecock that, Ali Khan explained, had been a legend in his day and that he had won at cards from a drunken deserter from the Russian Navy. The rooster's fighting spurs and the silver bells on his tiny cap glinted in the thin light of the harbormaster's second lamp like a beacon beckoning me to I knew not what."

*"I knew not what . . . " What a load of crap this is,* the Captain thinks. *And now it's time for a sip of water.* He drinks.

"I paused to see what other objects I could make out. Besides Old Lucifer, I could see nothing through the gloom except six glass jars atop Ali Khan's massive desk. Each was filled with sharpened pencils, even though the point of the pencil he was holding in his hand at that very moment was worn, hardly a point at all, as it hovered above a sheet of foolscap covered with images of crudely drawn dirigibles, each dropping a stream of egg-shaped bombs. The bombs' trajectories were represented by a series of dotted lines that stretched from the bellies of the dirigibles where they had been released to the plummeting bombs themselves."

The Captain speaks the word *bombs* with a special push, and is satisfied to see the audience straighten. *Nothing like the promise of violence to make the swine sit up*, he thinks.

■

And where *is* Louis? Jeffery wonders. Sometimes he pictures him shuffling his slippers down some dusty sidewalk outside the Burrow, wearing his sweater, lugging bags of groceries to whatever new abode he's found, and at other times he sees Louis on vacation, strolling to or returning from the beach wearing the same slippers he wore while in the Burrow, but now amid a flock of tanned and luscious bodies and without the sweater, because it's too hot for that. But most often in Jeffery's mind Louis is doing something simple, like trying on hats at the Mad Hatter's in the mall. Did Louis wear hats? The truth is that because he never saw the man outside the Burrow he has no idea, but a fedora would look good on him. *Louis should wear a hat*, Jeffery thinks. *It's not too late. Or is it?*

■

"'Mon cher Captain,' Ali Khan said," the Captain tells his audience, "'it is a very great pity, but with our newly installed government many, many additional forms have arrived, and these will need to be completed before you can leave the port. I hate to mention it, but it is no longer the old days, Captain, when a person such as you could arrive and sail out in a single afternoon. With all these new forms to be dealt with, I cannot imagine you departing before a week has passed, perhaps five days at the very soonest.'

"As Ali Khan took a sip from a filthy glass of ghastly colored liquid and awaited my reply, I studied him. He was thin, and his olive skin and dark hair reminded me of nothing so much as the breadsticks my mother used to bake and let me poke into a pot of prune jam when I was a boy.

"'But surely, Ali Khan,' I said, 'for an experienced manager such as yourself, there must be some way to expedite matters.' I stopped, omitting the perishable nature of my cargo. We both understood that in twenty-four more hours the fish aboard the *Shanghai Pearl* would be absolutely spoiled, and the ship's owners' fortunes ruined, and I didn't want to give him an extra card to display before me.

"Ali Khan shut his catlike eyes and pretended to be deep in thought. Then he opened them, one at a time, a trick that I later became familiar with in other offices of government officials in that part of the world—but whatever they hoped to accomplish by employing it I could never understand. He pretended to stare at a ceiling fan that, while impossible to see, I could hear churning its way through the darkness. Ali Khan returned his gaze to me, and said nothing. I had a good idea of what he was up to.

"'I wonder,' I suggested, 'if there is any way that you might be able to find someone you can trust—possibly a relative of yours—who might have a few free moments to ensure that the forms are correctly filled out. I would be willing to pay as much as one hundred dollars an hour if such a person could be found.'

"Ali Khan laughed, as if he found the possibility of such an original notion to be highly entertaining. Meanwhile, I crouched on my side of his massive desk like a tiger, a man-eater such as I often observed, who, too wounded or too old to hunt more challenging game, settles on the easiest prey of all, native flesh. Above us, the sounds of the fan struggled through the blackness, and outside the open window I could hear the cries of umbrella vendors hawking flimsy domes that had been hastily constructed out of palm leaves and plastic grocery bags. The two of us sat as still as the hand-carved statues of the Buddha that could be bought cheaply at the local market."

■

One night, after an especially late dance practice thanks to a few extra sessions at the barre, Ballerina Mouse is walking (no, limping) home, because at that hour the buses have all stopped running. Her foot hurts more than usual, and she's only about halfway home, passing through the part of town that is mostly vacant lots, when suddenly she sees a bright light in the sky overhead. It comes closer, and as much as she would like to hide, it seems as if she's somehow paralyzed. The next thing she knows, she's being pulled upward . . .

*No, this is stupid.*

■

The audience in the Masonic Hall is quiet, no doubt engrossed by the thought of another native eaten, this one by a tiger, not a bear. *This is going well*, the Captain thinks. He can almost feel his Death Quotient dropping by the minute, to what—maybe seventeen, or even twelve?

"And at last, after what seemed a long time, Ali Khan spoke from a sort of twilight reverie. 'Cher Captain,' he said, 'I have recalled my entire *family tree* (as I believe is the term used by you Westerners), on the sides of both my father and my mother, and I am sorry to report that all the fruits of its various branches are at present engaged in important business; otherwise I am sure they would be only too happy to help. It is an honor, to be sure, to be a member of such a talented and educated family, but it unfortunately means there are no available *deadbeats*—a curious word, if I am using it correctly—who can be pressed into such a service as you demand at a moment's notice. I myself, as you can see, am kept constantly busy by the pressures of my office. Nor, for obvious reasons, is it permitted for you to complete the forms yourself.'

"As he spoke, I could see the pleasure these words gave him. Meanwhile, I reached into my sea bag and removed a bottle of liquor similar to the one that was already open, but one whose contents were of a slightly less reprehensible hue. I placed it next to the first on his desk. Saying nothing, Ali Khan ran a finger over his narrow mustache, as if the bottle had arrived on his desk of its own accord and he was now waiting to see what it would do next."

■

*What, if anything, might have prepared Raymond for his residence in the Burrow?*

Basements, certainly, and closets. Swimming underwater. Reading by flashlight a book under the covers. Linen chests. Caves. Cardboard boxes. Crawling inside cardboard boxes and closing the flaps behind him. Crawling inside cardboard boxes and closing the flaps behind him, then sealing them from the inside with packing tape. Crawling inside cardboard boxes and closing the flaps behind him, then sealing them with packing tape and shutting his eyes. A baby duck he once had as a pet when he was young.

■

*What has prepared Heather for her life in the Burrow?*

Sleep, being hit over the head once in sixth grade and losing consciousness for a minute, waking up to find out someone had pushed her off the swings.

*A life made of air.*

■

The Captain winks at the audience to let them know that they don't have to worry about the outcome of this particular battle of wits. As usual, after his speech and the subsequent Q & A, there will be some kind of program, an installation of new officers, the handing out of trophies, and certificates of merit, and plaques—a whole industry based solely on vanity—and as usual, he'll sneak out before that gets started.

The Captain returns to his story: "'I understand you entirely, Ali Khan, and it was precisely because of the rest of your family's talent that I had hoped to find a suitable person to fill in the forms in question.'"

He pauses to let his audience absorb this thought, then continues. "In response, Ali Khan gave me an insincere smile and poured some of my gift into a fresh filthy glass. The man filled it halfway, studied it, and topped it off with more liquor from the bottle he had been drinking from earlier. For what seemed an eternity, the two of us watched the color change from green to light blue. Then Ali Khan placed one of his slender fingers in the liquid, removed it, lifted it into his mouth, and kept it there, evidently appreciating the intermingling of the two alcohols with his own sweat and God knows what else may have been beneath the nail of that unspeakable digit. At last he removed his finger from his mouth and wiped it on the blotter of his desk, which was marked, I could see, by many similar stains.

"Seeming to ignore me, Ali Khan returned to his drawings, adding several more bombs, and also three more lighter-than-air craft. These new bombs, I observed, appeared designed not to kill or maim, but were apparently aimed solely at groups of large-breasted women, with the bomb's sole mission being to remove their blouses. I watched as Ali Khan filled sheet after sheet with undressed women. Meanwhile, I knew the ice atop my fish was melting."

The Captain pauses and takes another sip of water, not because he is thirsty—he's endured far worse than this—but to let the drama of the slowly ripening cargo of fish sink in. He guesses he has four, maybe five more years of making a living this way and then he'll have to think of something else. Maybe a blog: "The Captain's Table."

■

*And Junior? Is he doing some project with his crossbow about now, or what?*

He is not. Not at this moment, anyway.

■

Likewise, it is also possible to think you have touched a thing when you have not, and to believe you have remained untouched when this is not the case.

■

"At that moment," the Captain says, "Ali Khan looked up at me. 'My dear Captain,' he said, accompanying his words with a sort of smirk, 'forgive me, but I just remembered. It seems I have a certain successful cousin whose specialty is surgery of the brain, and most important, in terms of our current problem, he is at present under disciplinary suspension for neglecting to wash his hands before he operates. I have known my cousin—Piggy, as I call him—since we both were children, and in addition to being a surgeon, I can promise you he excels at filling out government forms. What do you say I ring him up and see if he has any free time?'

"'That would be excellent,' I told him.

"'In that case, there is one small matter we need to discuss,' said Ali Khan.

"I pretended I didn't already know what he had in mind. 'What is that?'

"'It is this,' he said. 'While I am sure your initial estimate of one or two hundred dollars an hour is more than generous for an ordinary person—indeed, it would seem a fortune to a person such as myself— for my cousin, who is a professional man and whose usual fees are far greater, he would surely consider such a modest amount to be an insult.'

"'How much do you think he would consider fair?' I asked.

"'To take just one example,' said Ali Khan, 'his fee for a simple lobotomy, which takes only about thirty minutes, start to finish, is the equivalent of five hundred US dollars and, even as quickly as Piggy works, it is my professional opinion you will need a minimum of five hours to complete such paperwork.'

"'Ah,' I said. 'And Piggy, when he performs his surgeries, does he give his patients any anesthesia?'

"'Of course,' said Ali Khan.

"'In that case,' I said, 'assuming that the anesthesiologist charges three hundred dollars an hour, then wouldn't Piggy's rate actually be closer to seven hundred dollars per hour?'

"'An interesting point,' Ali Khan replied. 'Let me discuss it with Piggy.' And from somewhere beneath his papers he pulled out a black, old-fashioned dial telephone, dialed, spoke an incomprehensible dialect into the receiver, then listened, spoke, and listened again. At last, putting a hand over the mouthpiece, he turned to me and said, 'Piggy says his anesthesiologist only charges one hundred an hour.'"

The Captain pauses and looks out over the crowd. *They are mine*, he thinks, *my audience*, with the possible exception of one agitated individual, a bearded throwback from another era wearing a kind of lumberjack shirt of black-and-red plaid who is pacing in the back of the room. *Possibly some kind of psychopath?* The man looks slightly familiar, but the Captain has no idea where he's seen him—if he has. He stands up straighter, then delivers the one line that never fails to elicit applause, a line that has already made its way into the public discourse even though most of its users are unaware of the source: "'Then you tell Piggy he should get a better anesthesiologist.'"

Laughter. Applause. Death Quotient: practically zero.

■

But never zero, because a thing can't be zero, can it?
*Can it?*

■

At this very moment Jeffery is alone in his room at the Burrow, listening to the faint sounds of grinding and thinking about the deep sadness of all stories, including his own life's narrative. A story is born—his own—a trajectory begun; and presto, in that instant a death foretold: the spot where the bullet of his existence will strike the earth is preordained. So every person's story, he thinks, ends in the murder of its hero and his, alas, is no exception.

Far better for Jeffery on nights such as these, is the freedom of confusion, of incoherency, even outright dementia and Alzheimer's, where, taking a seat on a train with one's back to the locomotive, a person looks out on an endless expanse of receded time, stares at shabby neighborhoods, looks down on people picking their noses in cars beneath the window, or gazes overhead at the incomprehensible schedules, the public service announcements, but never, never can see forward to a final destination. No, best of all is the rider who dozes, perhaps waking for a moment to say a word or two to the passenger next to him or to nobody, then falls again to sleep until the station arrives, or rather *the rider* comes to the station, and is taken by surprise because here it is—as if by magic—the city, the house, the Burrow.

*What a pretentious fuck you are*, Jeffery thinks. But still, if a person knows he is pretentious, then maybe he's not.

■

So the words have done their magic once again. The crowd comes to its feet with laughter and applause, and the Captain concludes his story by telling how he had to pay the so-called neurosurgeon only eight hundred dollars an hour, thus saving the shipping company a whole thousand dollars. His ship sailed that same afternoon and the cargo of precious tuna was saved.

After that, the usual Q & A follows without a hitch until the man wearing the lumberjack shirt, the same one the Captain noticed pacing in the back of the hall earlier, raises his hand and will not lower it until he is recognized to speak. "Yes?" the Captain finally asks. "What is it? Do you have a question?"

But instead of staying where he is, this man with beady blue eyes, who sports a beard that looks like a lemming has seized his lower jaw and is hanging on for dear life, walks straight to the front of the hall, not ten feet from the lectern where the Captain stands, and plants himself there, apparently struggling to say something that's important. For a fleeting second the Captain regrets having left the Walther back at the house.

But no, this is no ordinary assassin. There is no homemade bomb, no bullet, no knife. Instead, the question turns out to be much more dangerous. The stranger waits a moment longer, opens his mouth: "Is it true that in the year 1994 you were arrested on the set of an obscure television situation comedy called *Mellow Valley* for acts unbecoming a sea captain?"

■

Another theory is that the Burrow is not at all unique, but one of many such places. That unbeknown to the general public, several "outside parties," in some kind of a franchise operation, have quietly been purchasing any available small hill or mound of earth that might be easily turned into tenant housing, and then renting out apartments cheaply to occupants who are actually only "placeholders" until the actual intended tenants are moved in, a sort of Trojan horse, or series of Trojan horses that one night will open to reveal their true purpose.

But then, what is the true purpose of anything?

■

To the *St. Nils Eagle*

Dear Editors,

I wonder if your readers have an extra crossbow or two resting in a closet or stored on a shelf in their garage.

If the answer is yes, here's a chance to bring that old friend back to life!

As most people know, there are scores of former military personnel who, in the course of their service to this country, were injured either by an explosive device or maybe even friendly fire, and as a result have an understandable aversion to loud noises. Yet these brave men and women still possess the "killer instinct" and, finding nowhere to use it in a supportive environment, are often forced to resort to senseless violence and the like.

What better way to help satisfy the basic human needs of these gun-shy warriors than to put our old silent, deadly crossbows back to use? By doing so, you will not only help our veterans to "simmer down" but also provide a public service in the extermination of small rodents and other unwanted animals. Fight Quietly On (FQO.org) is now accepting donations of any crossbows (even slingshots) that you may be able to provide. Please give those weapons a new home by sending them to FQO, Apartment B, 111 Gonzales Ave., in St. Nils.

Thanking you in advance,
A Proud Fellow American

IX

■

Lately, at night, when Heather is lying alone in her bed, just before sleep, thinking about what she needs to do next in her life, she takes comfort in the faint sounds of the grinding in the earth outside the walls of the Burrow: dirt, rocks, stumps, roots, the dens of groundhogs, foxes, badgers, weasels, and rabbits, all being slowly chewed to nothingness between the teeth of some gigantic metal mouth while she is still safe, still special, beneath her covers, breathing. The total effect is far more peaceful than most people might guess.

■

Somewhere outside the Burrow, leaves from a tree that has no name are lying on the ground beneath it, ready to be tied back on.

*Hurry*, the leaves say, *hurry*.

■

"Special," Madeline says out loud in front of the mirror in the bedroom of her apartment, practicing for the interview she is sure she'll give one day. "That's what we all are, every last one of us, and just because I happen to be a celebrity, I hope you don't think I've forgotten my roots and also all the people who helped me on my way up to where I am now."

■

What can a person tell about another person simply by a look at his sock drawer? As it turns out, plenty. For one, are the socks just tossed in without regard to color or material, or is each pair rolled lightly at the tops so they stay together? For that matter, has each pair been rolled into a self-contained ball, like a sow bug, fearful of being separated from its mate—which, if you know anything about bugs—not even bugs, by the way, but crustaceans—doesn't make sense because a sow bug is a single bug, and its mate would be somewhere next to it in a ball of its own, wouldn't it? Do sow bugs even have mates? In any case, Viktor's socks, as you might imagine, are sow bugs.

And what else is in Viktor's drawer along with his socks? Eight silver dollars, four Indian head nickels, an extra calculator, a chrome nail clipper, a piece of coal, and an old cut-crystal doorknob that used to open the door of his bedroom in one of the foster homes he lived in. On his last day there he unscrewed it and hid it in his suitcase when he left.

Also, rolling around on the drawer's bottom (or rolling as best they can among the balls of socks) are fourteen marbles that represent the total of Viktor's marble collection, a project begun years earlier when one morning he found a blue-and-white swirled marble on the sidewalk in front of his old apartment and put it in his pocket, not thinking of it until that night, when, removing his trousers, he noticed it again and put it in his sock drawer. After that, the concept of having a collection of anything at all remained dormant in his brain for a long while. Then, one afternoon on his way to the hardware store to buy an extra deadbolt for his front door, he happened to look down to see another marble, this one a cat's-eye, at his feet. So he picked it up and, upon returning home, decided it might be an interesting start to a collection. From that point on, all he had to do was to "fill the gap" between the two marbles he now owned. In this way, he thinks, it is possible for a person who has started from nothing to gain control over his universe, or at least a part of it.

■

You know that scene in cheap horror movies where the hero, the victim—whoever—starts to hear a sound, a siren, that grows louder and louder and louder and then he is covering his ears with both hands, pressing into them as hard as he can, and still he can't make the sound go away, but it just keeps on getting louder?

It's a scene that Raymond often thinks about.

He thinks about it most often when he lies in bed at night listening to the grinding sounds coming from somewhere outside the Burrow.

■

Should Jeffery get back with Madeline again? Should he go the extra mile to topple Viktor and push him aside? In some ways he thinks that Viktor would be less formidable an opponent than Raymond, and, besides, he likes Raymond. But honestly, he can't decide. Sometimes Jeffery misses Madeline and sometimes he doesn't all that much. Passing Madeline in the hall he sometimes wants to say, "Hey, babe, do you remember when you and I had a special thing going on?" Then Jeffery will look at her again and think, *But did we?* What if back then she was only on the rebound from Louis, something she denied, but how can he be sure? And suppose Madeline hadn't been thinking that at all. He could ask her, certainly, but suppose Madeline started explaining all over again why she decided to leave him. *Don't go there, friend*, he tells himself. *Stay away from negativity. Think about solutions. Consider Heather.*

■

Another time when Viktor and Madeline are together, Madeline suddenly wakes in the middle of the night and begins to speak in a voice Viktor has never heard before, deep and growly, almost scary. "Viktor," she says, and it doesn't sound as if Madeline is talking to him, but instead to some unknown third person, "to be a celebrity means to be celebrated, and so my interest in them is purely definitional. In other words, if myself and others didn't care, then there wouldn't be any celebrities at all. On the other hand, it *is* because we care that they exist, and in this respect celebrities are our creations. *We* are the creative ones, not them."

Should he wake her, and if so, whom would he be waking, Madeline or the snarling and possibly dangerous person lying next to him? *Let well enough alone*, he thinks.

But wait, the voice has one more thing to add: "In other words, to be a celebrity, such as I soon plan to be, means that a person is not subject to the same laws as ordinary people. And you, Viktor, are as ordinary as, well . . . mud."

Is Madeline really asleep? She is asleep, although she may also be insane. To calm himself Viktor gets up and goes to the kitchen, where he drinks, straight from the carton, half of somebody's quart of milk. Then he comes back to bed. Madeline is still sleeping, quiet. *There are worse things in this world than mud*, he thinks. *A lot of them.*

■

When Junior reflects upon his long-gone acting career, he decides that the only upside to the humiliation it brought him is—thank goodness for small favors—that no one has ever put that show he was in, *Mellow Valley*—which turned out to be the sum total of his show business experience—back on the air as reruns.

That would be much too much.

∎

Jeffery imagines Louis trying on a hat, walking over to a mirror, shaking his head, tipping the brim down and squeezing the crown, then walking back to choose another one—maybe a porkpie or one with a wider brim. *Did Louis even own a hat?* Jeffery wonders. It doesn't matter; the man was made to wear them, and Jeffery can imagine a conversation they might have had, maybe in the kitchen, late at night, had Louis stayed.

"You were born to wear hats," Jeffery would have said.

And Louis would have answered, "Is that so? Thank you, Jeffery. I genuinely appreciate your advice."

∎

As far as Madeline can tell from her research on the Internet and elsewhere, there has never been a celebrity who lived in the Burrow, even for a short period of time when they were younger, before they became a celebrity. And so, at her lowest moments, she wonders if the Burrow might be some sort of a jinx, some bad luck, such that even a short stay in the Burrow—sleeping on a couch overnight, for example—would have the power to mess a person up so badly that no matter what she does after she leaves, no matter how good she becomes at whatever it is she wants to do—even if she develops a cure for cancer—still no one will ever hear about it and she will never ever become a celebrity. And Madeline has spent far more time here than a single night on someone's couch. When she thinks about it, she's been in the Burrow longer than anyone except Raymond. Who, by the way, ought to be the subject of some story, or at least an article in the *St. Nils Eagle* Sunday Supplement, regarding his talent for making decoys. In it, he could credit his success to her.

■

It's stories, Jeffery thinks, that are the heroin, the horse, the H, the big H, the candy, the crap, the doojee, the dope, the flea powder, the hard stuff, the junk, the mojo, the scag, the antifreeze, the brown sugar, the smack, the train, the tar, the sweet dreams, the addiction that keeps the poor old nag of the human race running around the track again and again—the promise that no matter how confusing things are, no matter how completely messed up and hopeless, even doomed, someday, somehow, everything will eventually make sense.

That's why people keep on going, Jeffery thinks: losers because of the promise of a dramatic turn in their fucked lives—some long-lost relative, an inheritance, a winning lottery ticket, some old girlfriend, some screenplay they've had in a drawer for years being sold for a million dollars—and meanwhile the winners persist because that same narrative keeps patting them on their backs. *You are so right*, that narrative says. *You did all the right things. You deserve to be praised. Congratulations.*

But how can he turn this whole narration business to his profit? That's the million-dollar question.

■

Raymond thinks about how a dog will smell his owner's shoe, remember the owner, and maybe track him down for miles. But without a shoe, or hat, or sock, what does that same dog think about his missing owner? Does the dog, while walking around his new owner's house, doing the things dogs do, smelling the dirt and scratching his fleas, remember the good times he used to have together with his old owner, maybe at the dog park or chasing squirrels? Or are such moments only saved up in his dreams, like when you go into a house you have never seen before and suddenly there is something, some table or a chair or painting that you know, and you ask yourself: *Where did that come from?*

In other words how does Madeline remember him?

Is he in Madeline's dreams?

■

To make matters worse, Heather thinks, what with all this talking on the phone—even wearing a headset so she can move when she wants to—she's not getting all that much exercise. There's a tiny ring of fat she can feel around her tummy, and though some guys might think it's cute, she knows it's best to start a new relationship without one. Once things get going, she figures, she can afford to add a pound or two, have a special dessert now and again.

First though, if she can ever get out of the Burrow, she'll need to join a gym or health club, but until then, well, she needs to come up with a way to keep in shape while staying in her room. She pauses to think. Hmm. What kind of exercise can one do in a relatively limited space? She thinks some more, and the answer arrives.

Yes. She'll take up yoga. In the future as she talks on the phone servicing her clients she can do all those different poses.

*Namaste, motherfuckers.*

■

Every so often Madeline thinks about those stupid decoys, how even though they were what made Raymond special, they also used to drive her fucking absolutely crazy because there she and Raymond would be, making love or whatever, and all of a sudden she would notice their tiny eyes all around her, eyes that were unable to see forward, but only to each side of their heads, and without being able to help herself she would think: *What would it be like to live like that?*

Even now, it's a thing she still wonders about.

Sometimes they come to her in dreams and, when they do, she wakes up screaming.

■

And also the intermittent touch, the one left and then returned to, the touch like notes from a piano coming from indoors and out into the air, already faded, fading.

■

| DECOYS | CELEBRITIES |
|---|---|
| Perform a service | Perform a service |
| Always smile | Always smile |
| Have no feelings | Hide their feelings |
| Are designed to float | Can float if necessary |
| Made of wood | Made of flesh |
| Help hunters | Help autograph hunters |
| Used for interior decoration | Used for exterior decoration |
| Pretend to be alive | Are usually alive |

X

■

Meanwhile, in another place, leaves from a different tree that has no name are lying on the ground beneath it, stacked in order of size, ready to be tied back on.

*Hurry up*, they say. *Get ready.*

■

Sometimes, standing in front of a mirror in the Burrow, Madeline likes to practice for all the interviews she'll have to give when she finally breaks into the celebrity chef business. "Madeline," they will ask, "what is your favorite dish?"

"Signature or classic?"

"Let's start with classic."

Then she'll shrug her shoulders modestly, as if she should know better but can't help herself. "You may be surprised to hear this, Bruce, but the fact is I like nothing better than a simple omelet, perfectly prepared.

The secret, if anyone cares to know, is only that you use the very best butter. I insist on butter that comes from Europe, where it is prepared using old-world methods, not the hurried modern ones that involve mixing in artificial color and other additives. And when people ask me, 'Madeline, where can a person find such butter if they live here in the United States?' I answer that fortunately they can find it for themselves in their own neighborhood supermarket, in the section called 'Cooking with Madeline.' And then I tell them if by any chance their supermarket doesn't have such a section, they should talk to the manager and demand they install one, pronto."

"Madeline, that is very helpful. Thank you so much. And now, out of all the fabulous recipes you have created, which would you consider to be your signature dish?"

Madeline laughs, glances at the lamp reflected in her mirror, and imagines it's a television camera. "That's a tough question to answer, but I suppose I would have to say the dish that has brought me most comment is my raspberry gumdrop tart, though I'm the first to admit that raspberry tarts and even gumdrops have been around for a long time. Until me, however, no one ever thought to put them together, and I find that the freshness of the fresh raspberries blends perfectly with the slightly sticky sweetness of the gumdrops (no mint, please!). The beauty of this recipe is that a person doesn't even have to add sugar because it's all in the gumdrops but, at the same time, be sure to cook the pastry portion of this dessert first (thirty minutes at three hundred fifty degrees), and then add the gumdrops and raspberries, because the raspberries should be nearly uncooked, and the gumdrops should be under the broiler only long enough to be glazed a little by the heat, not melted. If you aren't sure whether you have the kind of gumdrops that resist melting you can find them in the 'Cooking with Madeline' section of your supermarket, where you can also find my frozen tart pastry dough. If you want to try this for yourself, you can find the recipe at cookingwithmadeline.com."

■

Celebrity: a famous person. From the Latin *celeber*, meaning numerous, or much frequented.

■

"Do you have any regrets in your career as a successful chef? Is there anything you are still waiting to accomplish?"

Here a long silence follows. When Madeline finally comes back to the question it's obvious from the mirror that her expression has changed. She is visibly sadder, almost weary.

"As a chef, no. But when I see all the hungry people in this world, people for whom a half bowl of cooked rice would be a feast, people who sit around all day gnawing on roots and bark, people who have to slaughter their family dog, or cat, or even their canary in order to get a little protein, people who comb through the dumpsters and trash cans outside of Madeline's Gourmet Restaurants in search of some specks of crème brûlée, or for a smear of pâté someone has missed stuck to the bottom of a shred of lettuce, it makes me so unhappy.

"Also, Bruce, it may surprise you to learn there are people who are so hungry they consider themselves lucky if they come across a snake and beat it to death, or a toad, too, though with toads a person has to be careful, because there are several varieties that are extremely toxic, including the cane toad and the Asiatic toad, which, paradoxically, plays an important part in Eastern medicine, so if you get one of those and wolf it down without thinking just because you're starving, without having first looked it up in a book about those things—and frankly most people won't take the

trouble to do this—you could be dead or at least seriously ill. Then there are also insects, naturally, which a
person can roast after pulling off the wings and legs,
and they don't in fact taste too bad—sort of a nutty
taste, it seems to me—although I suggest you avoid the
ones with stingers—and unbelievably, there are also
people so desperate that they actually eat fleas—yes,
fleas!—which their womenfolk grind in a mortar until
they're dead and turn into a paste, and then the paste
is mixed with just a little tree sap—I forget the name
of the tree they use—to give it a little sweetness and to
hold it together—not too much, because the resulting
dish, called a "flea stick," is meant to be crunchy, not
chewy. And although it is true that because I am an
artist I have no choice but to follow my art wherever it
leads me, I still think it's important for everyone to remember that in the world there are a lot of people who
are destitute, miserable, and hungry as well, so even as
an artist, I constantly try to think of innovative and de-
lightful ways to please all palates, from the most sophisticated to the average, which is something I believe
we *all*—and not just celebrities—need to do more of."

"Thank you so much, Madeline."

"Any time, Bruce. Ready and waiting."

■

*But waiting for what?*
   *And waiting for how long?*

■

Jeffery watches Trisha Reed, the television news
reporter who is a celebrity in her own right, speak about
the sudden influx of strangers who have been seen
wandering about St. Nils. Trisha Reed has a friendly
but businesslike demeanor, as if at one time she was,
or had thought about being, a real estate agent. "People
report sightings of a mix of men and women," she says
and looks concerned, "but they are always described
as 'dirty,' and many at times are covered with what
witnesses call 'actual soil.'" Then Reed displays some
grainy photographs as evidence, holding them away
from her as if the dirt displayed on the pictures might
somehow be transferred to her fashionable scarlet dress
and well-coifed golden hair. The photos are hard to
make out; they are blurred and grainy, and could be
people, gophers, or anything, truly. "Even worse," Reed
adds, "these strangers do nothing in particular, have
nowhere they need to go, but walk the streets without

an apparent destination." She gives her head a smallish, outraged, attractive shake.

Jeffery scratches his own head. How could anyone possibly know someone else's destination?

"Authorities conjecture these people may be part of a drug smuggling operation that went wrong," Trisha Reed continues, giving her hair a flip to indicate that she is not responsible, even though this *is* a matter for public concern. "No one can say for certain," she reads from the prompter, "but on the other hand," (another flip), "the males appear not to be dangerous." She cautions, however, that citizens should not approach them, even to offer small gifts of food or bottles of water or moist towelettes, as has been reported happening in certain liberal neighborhoods. "Some of the females"— and here she manages to convey a sort of sneering tone without an actual sneer—"have been reported being seen in fancy restaurants dining with wealthy men." Then she reverts to her original expression of confused concern. It is also possible, she adds, that such individuals are not criminals at all, but victims of an illegal smuggling operation. However, while all our fellow humans in general should be treated with compassion, we should keep in mind that any victim can be dangerous if provoked, and the best thing a person can do is report any further sightings of these people as soon as possible to the authorities.

"We live in dangerous times," Trisha Reed says and looks hard into the lens of the television camera. "We all need to be vigilant."

■

Heather looks in her mirror. Her hair is okay, but not much more than that. In other words, nothing special, a mousey brown, a little limp, but not horrible by any means. Cut it off, the voice in the mirror says. You need to cut it off.

*The voice in the mirror?*

But right now her hair is just long enough that sometimes—frequently, in fact, while she's listening to guys on the phone tell her what they want to do to her—she can take one end and put it in her mouth to suck on while she passes the time until they've finished with wherever their wishes take them (often, nowhere good).

Would Raymond like her better with short hair?

■

*Is* Viktor making as much money from his numerous investments in the stock market as he claims? Jeffery wonders. If so, he's some kind of genius, and possibly the most successful investor in all of history. But if that *is* the case, why is he still living in the Burrow? *Or*, could it be, as someone—Raymond? Madeline?— once suggested as a joke, that Viktor is no investor at all, but a drug lord lying low inside the Burrow until the gangland war going on aboveground dies out. Also, could Viktor's presence here be somehow related to those so-called wandering strangers on the news? Is it possible they are not strangers at all, but hired assassins looking to put "a hit" on Viktor? Did the strangers exist before Viktor's arrival?

*Or*, taking a different approach, *could* Viktor have been placed in the Burrow as a part of the Federal Witness Protection Program? Is the Burrow actually what they call in espionage parlance a "safe house"? If so, is Jeffery the only one who doesn't feel particularly safe?

And by the way, what *is* going on with all those sounds of grinding coming from the earth? Why doesn't everyone think this is a problem? Could this new activity be related to the sudden influx of strangers? Is it possible, as sometimes happens in science fiction movies, that these noises have disturbed some

long-buried race of monsters who are now coming up
to the surface? As interesting as this thought may be,
Jeffery doubts it's true.

■

In Raymond's most recent dream Viktor and Madeline
are standing next to a float left over from the Founding
of St. Nils Day, a day celebrated every year with a
parade that features several floats in the form of ducks
(Could that be why Raymond chose St. Nils to settle
in?), because, indeed, the city was founded after its first
settlers followed a flight of waterfowl to a quiet marsh
at the edge of the sea.

In his dream, however, the parade has long since
been over, and Madeline and Viktor, dressed in black,
are wielding axes as they hack apart one of the larger
floats, a fairly accurate representation of a blue-winged
teal. It's a male, with the usual slate-colored head, white
crescent band behind its bill, blue-gray inner wings,
light-brown flight feathers, and brown speckles on its
body, only it's about eighteen feet tall. As they work,
they turn to Raymond.

"Look," Viktor shouts, "we have an extra axe," and
sure enough, there is an extra axe lying against the

bumper of the vehicle the float was built on top of, now exposed by their hacking.

"Yes," Madeline adds, "and when we're done, I'll cook it all up into a nice stew for us to eat."

Raymond starts to explain that it goes against his innermost nature to take up arms against a duck and, besides, because the float is made of wood and wire, plus other materials, he's pretty sure it won't be good to eat, but before he gets a chance to say anything, Madeline walks up to him and puts an axe in his hands.

"Raymond," she says, "if you love me you *must* do this."

Against his better judgment, Raymond takes it, shuts his eyes, and swings.

■

"So, Junior," Tammy is saying, "why don't you tell me something positive that happened this last week?"

Tammy's favorite word is *positive* and Junior hates it. Today she is wearing a charcoal turtleneck and a dark skirt that makes her look smaller than she is, although she is pretty small. The ankh is gone, and in its place is a shiny gold necklace where the links are in the shape of jumping fish, kind of like he's seen on the backs of old guys' RVs, but these are a lot more elegant, at least when Tammy's wearing them, and if she's angry about the fact that he was late to his appointment, she's not showing it, except maybe by the way she is clamping down on her pen.

"Well," Junior says, and stops to think, because this being positive is truly a burden, "as I was driving here a cat ran out in front of my car, but I managed to swerve just in time, which was good because it was a momma cat, and she was carrying a kitten in her mouth." He's taking a wild guess that Tammy is a cat lover.

"And yet you still missed the time for your appointment by a whole ten minutes," Tammy says with a cute, ironic smile.

Or course, Junior has made up the story about the cat. There wasn't any cat or any other animal, and the day he'll stop for one, that will be the day, all right, so now he's glad he told a lie because it proved Tammy *had* been angry about his being late and, when you think about it, ten minutes is nothing in the course of a lifetime. He can feel a twinge inside his stomach—a sure sign that what he likes to call his Rage Meter is on its way up.

"But let's not dwell on that," Tammy says. She crosses, then uncrosses her legs, and her stockings make the tiniest scritch. "Remember your homework for the week—to imagine a happy moment you might have had with your father, the one you told me was a sea captain, if he had stayed around to raise you."

"Well, I'm not one hundred percent sure he was a captain," Junior says. "I mostly just think that. I don't know why but I do."

"Don't change the subject," Tammy says. "I was asking you about your homework."

"Sorry," Junior says. "It's gone. I guess the cat ate it. I mean, just kidding. I've been kind of busy."

"With what?"

"Oh, sports. The archery thing," says Junior.

■

Safe or not, the truth is that Jeffery sees the Burrow as only temporary, a stopping place, or maybe more accurately, a pausing place, on the road to where he wants to go. So if Viktor is a drug lord, or even if he makes as much money as he claims to, well, let him, Jeffery thinks. It's only temporary.

But where *does* Jeffery want to go from the Burrow? That's the question. At what point on the axis of his life will the Present Jeffery finally intersect with the Future

Jeffery, the one he's certain he's on his way to meet?
And needless to say, when he does join him, the Future
Jeffery will be 1) sexually magnetic but not obsessed;
2) well-read but not a nerd; 3) moderately good at all
sorts of sports and board games, too, but not too much
of a fan—he'll be much too busy with his own career to
waste time that way. The Future Jeffery also will be 4)
well-groomed but not a fop; 5) kind to animals (which
reminds him that down here in the Burrow it's been
ages since he's seen an actual animal, even a bug); 6)
will have an appreciation for the arts and finer things,
including dining, in part thanks to Madeline; 7) be an
excellent judge of wine but never drink to excess; 8) will
always be happy to lend a hand if he has the time; 9)
will believe in socialism; and 10) will have a job . . . well,
not a job, exactly, but an inclination to do things that
bring him the approval of others, especially beautiful
women, which, coincidentally, will also happen to make
him a lot of money. But how *will* the Future Jeffery be
born out of the present, Present Jeffery? How are all
these things going to be achieved? Actually, it's not so
obvious. Because it's way too late for medical school,
and even if he wanted it—which he doesn't—to prepare himself for such a life of wealth and compassion
would mean Jeffery would have to go back, maybe as

far as the third or fourth grade, and retrain himself to direct his thoughts along more scientific lines. Business doesn't interest him at all—or investing—that he'll leave to Viktor. Being a rock star is out of the question. Jeffery has no musical aptitude whatsoever.

Architecture? No. Geography? No. Then what about being a writer? Hmm. But what kind of a writer? Books are hard and take too much time; poetry is fast enough, and easy, but not exactly an income stream. He thinks more. How about a screenplay, maybe for some block-buster movie? Good, but movies tend to be a one-time thing; there's a big payoff, and then nothing; you're back taking lunches and pitching projects along with every amateur in the neighborhood. How about a long-term project, say, like a television dramatic series—or better, a sitcom. *Now, that's a thought*, he thinks. That way he can sell the first season, make a little money, and then keep writing, churning them out for the next five or six years, and even while he is writing the next season's shows, can dream up new projects and pitch them, because, hey, nothing lasts forever. Except for the deep pockets of reruns.

But a sitcom about what? Crime? Too crowded. Lawyers? Ditto. Doctors, spies? Ditto. A doctor who is a spy and steals secrets while his patients are babbling under anesthesia? Is that against medical ethics? Maybe not, but where would he start? Wait a minute. Something is coming to him, an obscure sitcom he used to watch when he was a kid, called something like *Pleasant Valley*, or *Happy Valley*—something—about a bunch of hippies living on a farm somewhere in bumfuck nowhere. *You could do that*, he thinks. But wait! What if any of that show's creators are alive? Could they sue him for plagiarism? Does plagiarism even exist on television? It can't possibly, but what if it does?

So how about this? How about a bunch of people, Jeffery thinks, like Viktor, who are all in the Federal Witness Protection Program, and who, unknown to each other, all wind up living in a sort of an underground commune they call the Burrow. Why not? Write what you know. And if it works, it will make him enough money to get him out of here once and for all. Maybe enough to buy a house with a big front lawn and a gardener. He's always liked the idea of having a gardener. *Clip this. Trim that.* Once a month he'll get a bill and then, when he does, he'll be able to pay it, too. He can sense the Future Jeffery just on the other side of the door, waiting to be let in.

■

Time passes, with Ballerina Mouse appearing only in recitals in the most minor roles: in *Swan Lake*, she plays a duckling, in *The Nutcracker*, a slice of fruitcake. "But you are so talented," her fellow students tell her. "We have no idea why Mme. Suzanne isn't casting you in better parts." When they think she's not watching, she catches them laughing at her.

Then, one day she wins a public radio subscriber giveaway. She's not a subscriber, but the rules say you don't have to subscribe to be entered into the sweep-stakes, and so she wins a free trip to . . . Poland! And once she's there, having been asked by someone she meets at the ballet if she has any hobbies, she obliges with a few shy dance steps, and in no time finds herself the toast of Warsaw, where its residents, having been forced for years to watch so much ordinary, everyday dancing, beg her to stay so she will teach them how to emulate her unique and exquisite technique.

*Fat chance.*

■

The kitchen of the Burrow is not large. In fact, it's smaller than the kitchens of many ordinary houses, especially considering that at times (though not at this time, because the room where Louis lived is vacant) there are potentially six people occupying the apartments in the Burrow and thus using the kitchen. As kitchens go, it's fairly clean, though the kitchens used by several different people are seldom as clean as those where there is one person and one person only designated to use it. In the Burrow, Madeline is mostly in charge; however when other people drop in to cook something, or maybe warm up leftovers, usually late at night, they frequently—no, usually—leave behind a mess.

There is just one entrance to this kitchen, and on the wall a person faces when he or she steps through the entrance, arranged from left to right, are a stove and a stainless-steel sink. Above the stove and the sink are cabinets. The stove, as mentioned earlier, has a mirror behind it, tilted slightly downward, so sometimes when a person is cooking, it seems as if she is cooking as a team with someone else, whose face she can't see, only her hands. There are cabinets on the other three walls as well, and counters beneath them on which rest a microwave, a toaster oven, and a blender, in case anyone wants to make him or herself a smoothie or a milk shake. Beneath the counters are more cabinets and drawers.

The kitchen table has a gray Formica top and chrome legs, and is technically designed to seat four, because there are four matching chairs that are usually around it, but someone has added two extra chairs, one red and one blue, with the paint on the red one chipped. They usually are kept in the corner of the kitchen opposite the refrigerator unless they're needed, which mostly they are not because, as Jeffery pointed out earlier when he discussed his scheme for regular meetings, it's rare for everyone to be together in the kitchen, or anywhere in the Burrow, at the same time. The table has a drawer on one side with a chrome knob. The drawer holds a pair of pliers and a screwdriver, plus a few screws. Almost certainly if anyone needed a pair of pliers or a screwdriver in an emergency they would be out of luck because most people have forgotten it's even there, let alone what's inside. It would be the last place they'd think of looking.

The floor of the kitchen is covered with gray vinyl tile embossed in a wavy pattern to look like stone, but it fools no one. Floors like this were popular back in the days the Burrow was built. The cabinets are pine, though they have darkened with age, and they have white porcelain knobs, some of which are chipped. The walls are the brownish yellow of old vellum.

In other words, this kitchen is not the kind of kitchen you sometimes see in designer kitchen stores or on cooking shows but, as Madeline says, "I'm the only one who ever really uses it, so everyone else should shut up and stop complaining." Not that they do complain, because they don't, but in case they are thinking of it, they had better think again.

■

## ANOTHER SCENE FROM THE TECHNICAL SECTOR

**Tech #1:** Shit, shit, shit. It looks like there's another cave-in on Seven.

**Tech #2:** What? I thought they took care of that just last week.

**Tech #1:** Well now there's another.

**Tech #2:** Is it my imagination, or are things worse now that they've stopped using the old machines?

**Tech #1:** I don't know, but I think it has more to do with their planning than with the machines.

**Tech #2:** Maybe, but Seven is an old tunnel. It was planned a long time ago, before I came, anyway.

Tech #1:    Well, something is wrong. Have you seen the bit in the TV news?

Tech #2:    Sure, but you know that will die down soon enough, just like the last time.

Tech #1:    Probably, but I have to say I like the way that Trisha chick gets all bothered. She's a honey.

Tech # 2:   You think so? Honestly she just seems average to me.

XI

■

*Okay*, Jeffery thinks, *the first episode of The Burrow will introduce the characters—maybe a theme song, too.* The song should be something significantly hip, not one of those old-fashioned ones that try to summarize the entire premise of a show in three or four embarrassing verses—well—it should do that, but be ironic, too, and also the music for *The Burrow* should be tougher, almost scary—no, totally scary—Jeffery decides. That way it will be a relief when people get to know the characters, who might seem menacing at first, but will turn out to be funny and harmless, full of plans that fall apart, big ideas that go nowhere, and a ton of eccentric behaviors, as well.

Who are these people going to be? *Well,* Jeffery thinks, *write what you know.* Therefore, they should be the people who already inhabit where he's currently staying, the real-life Burrow. And of course, by the time the series is picked up by a major network, he'll be long out of here, so he won't have to listen to their complaints.

So start with Jeffery, a smart, charismatic go-getter who is trying to better his present situation. He's a likeable wise guy who always has big ideas, but so far, he's had one piece of tough luck after another through no fault of his own, and as a result these ideas have always fallen flat. Then there's Heather, the cute, ditzy girl who has a heart of gold and is looking for a career in show business, though it will be clear to the audience that she doesn't have a chance. This, he figures, will add a layer of depth to the show for those smart enough to see the contextual dissonance, because the whole time a sophisticated viewer will get that she *is* in show business, and can't be that much of a loser because, obviously, she *has* a show—this one—so the whole concept will be one of reality over art, with life not imitating art for once, but at the same time, it's the loser-girl people are falling for, not the actual actress playing her. But if people don't understand it, it won't get in the way. That's all right. It's not a deal breaker.

Naturally, there's Viktor—with a *K*, no less—so there will be a lot of laughs every time he corrects people about how to spell his name. Viktor will be a control freak, an anal kind of creep, but sincere in his way, and obsessive, too, which is a good thing because it will lead to other jokes when he can't stop repeating certain actions, and this will somehow feed into the spelling-of-his-name business. Should he also have Tourette's? That could be a little much for the first episode. Maybe it would be better to introduce it, say, midseason, and it could start mildly and get worse. Does Tourette's come on gradually or all at once? Note to self: *check out Tourette's symptoms*. Or maybe it could be some other weird disease, like a bowel condition, so there could be a lot of jokes about that.

Who else? Raymond, the lovable doofus, kind of out of it, but with a natural sense of what's really going on. An idiot savant, probably, and he can be doing something totally useless, collecting stamps or, better, comic books. He can have stacks of comic books filling his apartment, because he's a hoarder, too. His whole living room is nothing more than an aisle between towering stacks of comics at this point, but every once in a while one of them will turn out to be worth a zillion dollars, and he'll sell it to pay for an operation someone needs, or to buy a coffin for somebody's parent so they can be buried in peace after everyone else has given up hope. Not ducks though. People won't relate to ducks.

Then there's Madeline: she's like the Earth Mother of the place—kind of Anna Magnani crossed with Bette Midler—a redhead, naturally, a passionate individual with a big heart, but also wisecracking and cranky. She's the one the other people come to with their problems, but does she have anyone to talk to about her own seeming inability to stay in any relationship for more than a little while, an inability that possibly borders on—*say it!*—sex addiction? No. So she's an Earth Mother, although in the end she remains a lonely and tragic figure. Not bad.

But he also needs somebody he doesn't already know—some wild card who will give him the artistic freedom to bring in new themes, outside influences, guest artists.

Who . . . ? And then it's clear: a landlord. Somebody who can come in and stir things up every so often by hiking the rent or complaining that the residents aren't taking care of things, or that one of them—Heather, of course—is keeping a kitten she's not allowed to have. A landlord who is colorful, but not too colorful, a retired person, a retired military man, a sea captain, for example, a guy who's been around the world and has a lot of experience, but who's getting old and comically fails to understand the ways of the younger generation.

Mostly he'll be wandering around oblivious to what's happening, so everyone can laugh at him, but then every so often, he'll freak them all out by being wise, and save their asses. He'll have a wooden leg like Ahab, too. Perfect.

So start with an episode that introduces the characters, though not too many all at once, but allows each one to make his or her own entrance, one at a time, like the opening of James Joyce's story "The Dead," which Jeffery read back in high school and which was also made into a fairly successful movie with Angelica Huston, directed by her father, if he remembers correctly.

*Knock knock.*

*Who's there?*

*Mister About-to-be-a-Celebrity*

■

"Raymond, you ruffle my feathers," Madeline used to say to him once upon a time and, even if she was kidding, to hear her say it made him happier even than carving all those beautiful decoys made him happy, which was very, very much. *You ruffle my feathers*, and she'd be kissing him here and there and laughing, with

him and not at him, and he would be shy, but not shy
in another way, and soon all his skin, and even the skin
beneath his skin would be tingling, and then, Madeline
never being one for ceremony, her clothes would be
off—her bra, her stockings—tossed over a canvasback,
redhead, or mallard—Raymond's clothes, too, would
be on the floor—and he'd be touching her, as soft
as down, and he couldn't imagine how she could do
that, but she did, and then the two of them would be
touching each other so that after a while it was hard to
tell who was who, what part of the touch was Raymond
and what part was Madeline, and there would be the
sweat and the hair and he wasn't sure whose of what
was whose, and then almost without thinking he would
find himself inside her—or she would be around him,
however that went—so they were one moving thing,
like a duck and the water beneath the duck, the duck
in the water and the reflection of the duck in the water,
and he wouldn't be thinking about anything but what
they were at that moment, not even who was who or
about what they were doing, only that they *were* doing
it and it could go on and on and on, and then, when
it could go on no longer, when it couldn't get any
better and they were just lying there, out of nowhere,
Madeline would start to sing to him, yes, would hold

Raymond's head against her breasts, and sing her old songs: old rock and roll songs, oldies but goodies, the top forty and top fifty, even those songs he had only half listened to when he was young, but then, thanks to Madeline, the songs would be again, back as fresh as ever—no, fresher—and there wasn't any time anymore, because even though the songs were from a long time ago, she was singing them at that very moment, so her songs were new too, the mirror of the old songs, and there was no place other than where he was, no place other than where they were, that is to say in the Burrow in bed with the ducks all around them, and there wasn't any ending because before a song would even end, Madeline would start a new one, in that same soft whispering voice, and how she did that Raymond never knew, and back then it seemed as if the songs would go on, not forever, quite—he knew that—but whatever was the next thing to it.

Does she do that with Viktor? Does she sing to him that way? He certainly hopes not.

■

## TRANSCRIPT OF ADDITIONAL
## CONVERSATION FROM TECHNICAL STAFF

**Tech #1:** What do you mean, "not yet"? They were supposed to be here three days ago. What's the holdup?

**Tech #2:** I think one of the tunnels might have collapsed.

**Tech #1:** That's great. That's just great. I certainly hope not. Because do you know who's going to be blamed for it? Take a guess: we are. We always are.

**Tech #2:** I know. It doesn't seem fair.

**Tech #1:** You can say that again. And do you know what else doesn't seem fair—these stupid hats we're forced to keep on at all times. They're like having a snail shell on your head. I mean—on our heads. And not only do they look stupid, but they make us look stupid, too. No offense.

**Tech #2:** None taken. But aren't they supposed to be some protection against the atmosphere down here, or air pressure, something like that? That's what I remember from our training.

| Tech #1: | Atmosphere? They told the group I was with that they were supposed to cushion the skull in case of collapse. And I think they also said there was some kind of automatic oxygen supply inside. |
|---|---|
| Tech #2: | You could be right. I halfway remember them saying something about not walking too close to an open flame, or an open something. But do you know what I hate the most? |
| Tech #1: | What do you hate the most? |
| Tech #2: | I hate the fact that we have to keep them on. |
| Tech #1: | Day and night. |
| Tech #2: | Awake and sleeping. |
| Tech #1: | Yes, and on top of wearing the hats day and night, and on top of having to be sure all these people get where they are going when they're supposed to be there. |
| Tech #2: | Right. On top of that, what? |
| Tech #1: | On top of that, now there's the problem with the Burrow, too. |

∎

*Today it is snowing*, Junior thinks, though in reality it isn't, because it never snows in St. Nils. It's only snowing in the part of his mind that sees the world as unhappy because he is unhappy. And yes, he knows there are many who say the world is neither happy nor unhappy, but how are we supposed to know anything at all about the outer world except through our inner world? So if we are unhappy, then it's just too bad for the world, because what is the world good for, anyway? He likes how it feels to think these thoughts.

Or not, because this much thinking makes things even worse, thinks Junior, as when he thinks he has a thorn in his foot and the world won't get back to being okay again until it's removed, and people can talk about it all they want, can tell him to think about this or that, but still that thorn has got to come out. *Now,* Junior thinks, *who in this case put the thorn in my foot in the first place?*

That's easy: it was that captain, the old guy they brought onto the set of *Mellow Valley*, the asshole who was supposed to advise the actor playing an old sea captain in the episode where he wanders onto the farm and thinks he's at sea. That guy—not the actor, who was okay, but that captain hired to advise the actor—being a sea captain, couldn't help but remind him of Junior

Senior, the father he never knew, whose child-rearing strategy was essentially the same as a carp's: spawn and leave; spawn and get the hell out, because however much of a dumbass he may have been, clearly he had some incorrect premonition that his child would be even more worthless, and no matter how many awards (none) Junior ever won in junior (ha!) high school, it would never be enough to tip the scale where Senior (if he ever heard about them) would understand that he had made a mistake back then. But he was wrong: Junior is not a loser, a creep, a gimp, a nerd, a doofus. No. Junior is a real man. He'll show him. If not now, soon. Junior is through with all of Junior Senior's bullshit.

And okay: so he knows the old guy, this captain, *wasn't* his actual father, but when that asshole was on the set of *Mellow Valley*, he certainly acted like he was, making fun of Junior and pointing out his faults to other members of the cast, including, most importantly, to Heather. But even though he called the old man out in public at that alleged *lecture*, the man never even tried to answer his charges, and before Junior knew what was happening the old guy's henchmen had dragged him outside and told him never to show up again. Honestly, even thinking about it makes Junior want to shoot someone, not with a gun, of course, but with something quieter and just as deadly at close range—say, Old Stag Killer.

What would his therapist, Tammy, say if she knew? Junior wonders.

But of course he'll never tell because if he did she'd say he's a sicko; that's what she would say.

She'd say, "Back to the nuthouse for you."

■

Episode One, *The Burrow*, Scene One

Scary theme music plays.

An empty, darkened kitchen. Through a door, left, two men enter. Their faces are turned away from the camera as together they slowly walk to the refrigerator. VIKTOR makes the gesture "after you," in a way that seems mocking. The other man, named JEFFERY, opens the refrigerator door and takes out a carton of milk. Then, going to a cabinet, JEFFERY takes down a box of sugarcoated cereal. He fills a bowl, takes it to the table, and silently starts to eat. Meanwhile, VIKTOR rummages around in the refrigerator until he finds an open pack of cheese enchiladas. He takes it out and

puts it in the microwave. While waiting for the microwave to signal that the enchiladas are heated, VIKTOR
paces. When the oven makes its tiny beep, he removes
the pack, leaving behind a smear of cheese on the counter, takes out a fork, and joins JEFFERY at the table.

| | |
|---|---|
| **Viktor:** | Have you ever seen a rat trapped in a card-board box? |
| **Jeffery:** | What kind of cardboard box? Are you thinking about those that four six-packs of soft drinks come in, or more like this cereal box, something skinny that you can close at the top? |
| **Viktor:** | No. What I had in mind was the kind of box that holds several packages of toilet paper, or possibly paper towels—a big one, with high sides. |
| **Jeffery:** | No, I haven't. |
| **Viktor:** | Well, let me tell you about it. The first thing a rat will do in that situation is to jump around in every direction and try to find a way out. |
| **Jeffery:** | Are you sure? I remember back when I was a kid I went to a pet store once and the owner let one crawl all over me. It was |

|  | white and had brown spots. It was nice but my mother wouldn't let me have it. I must have been around ten ... |
|---|---|
| Viktor: | I'm not talking about tame rats. I'm talking about wild rats, the kind you see in sewers and in garbage dumps. Big, fierce ones. They're usually brown or gray. |
| Jeffery: | Okay, I thought you meant tame ones. So what are you saying? |
| Viktor: | I'm saying that when, after a while, after a rat has finished jumping around and he finally understands he can't get out, do you know what he will do? |
| Jeffery: | No. |
| Viktor: | He goes to a corner—it doesn't make a difference which one, because they're all the same in a box—and he puts his back against the wall, and then he turns and bares his fangs. |
| Jeffery: | His fangs? Do rats have fangs? |
| Viktor: | Well, his teeth. He bares his teeth. |
| Jeffery: | So why are you telling me this? |

Enter HEATHER, who is wearing a short nightgown and fluffy slippers.

**Heather:**    Oh, sorry guys. I didn't mean to disturb your man-talk.

**Jeffery:**    No problem. I was just leaving.

**Viktor:**    Me too. I was just leaving, too.

The men rise and leave their dirty plates on the table. VIKTOR takes a long look at HEATHER, before exiting, as if he is deciding something. JEFFERY just walks out. HEATHER picks up the plates and puts them in the sink. She washes them and places them in the drying rack to dry. She shakes her head.

**Heather:**    Did I do something wrong? I was going to have the enchiladas I was saving, but now I'm not so hungry.

■

Going from one mediocre celebrity dinner after another makes the Captain almost long for those sickening buffets back at sea—those endless fancy platters displaying dead animals, dead fish, dead grasses ripped from the earth—not so different, come to think of it, than having to repeat the same stories again and again, waiting for the audience to laugh at the same lines, in the same places. What kind of life is that for a real man, a man who is basically a man of action? The Captain tries to remember the last truly good time he had. Was it running down that boat full of so-called sightseers in Rangoon harbor? Standing, lashed to the wheel, during that typhoon in the China Sea? And on land? Possibly working as a technical advisor to that silly show about hippies. It was ridiculous, but at least there were lots of pretty girls, and the pay was good, despite the smart-asses in the production crew, that idiot of a director, and that infuriating kid, Junior something. That is, until what happened at the very end.

He can feel his Death Quotient starting to climb.

■

Get yourself a plan, thinks Madeline. Do this logically. Find a mirror and stand in front of it. Pretend you are being interviewed. Start with a question and go from there. Ready, set—

| Question: | What is it you like to do? |
| Answer: | I like to cook. |
| Question: | Then why not open a restaurant? |
| Answer: | Well, it takes money, for one thing. |

**Question:**   So you could start small. Maybe you could prepare food for others until you get famous enough that someone will give you money to start your own restaurant, and that person will be your first investor.

**Answer:**   Well, I already prepare food for others down here. Just the other day, for example, I made a really excellent artichoke and bacon quiche, and did anyone thank me?

**Question:**   No, but I'm sure it was appreciated. How about Viktor?

**Answer:**   What about him?

**Question:**   He claims to be making a ton of money. He should be able to spring for a restaurant.

**Answer:**   Viktor? That cheapskate? Are you kidding?

■

"I don't know what's happening to me," Madeline says to Heather. They are both in the kitchen, late at night. Heather is having her usual tea and arrowroot crackers, while Madeline is reheating a can of mushroom soup to which she has added a few spices to pick up the flavor.

"What's wrong?" Heather questions.

"I don't know," Madeline says. "Has this ever happened to you: you try to think of an ingredient—not even a complicated one, like cardamom or clove or coriander—in a recipe you've made a thousand times, but then you can't remember which one you need, or if it's something else entirely, like cumin? I mean—I know they're different, but sometimes I have a hard time remembering exactly how they are different anymore. Honestly, I'm afraid my mind is slowly disappearing. I think maybe it's a sign it's time for me to get out of here."

"No," Heather says. "It never has."

■

## ANOTHER CONVERSATION FROM THE TECHNICAL STAFF

**Tech #2:**    You know, I have a question, but I don't know if it's the kind of question I should ask or not.

**Tech #1:**    How can you know until you ask it?

**Tech #2:**    Well, it's this: We've been working together down here for a long time and, speaking for me at least, I wonder if you've noticed that practically the only talks we ever have are related to this work.

Tech #1:   I have, but what else is there to talk about?

Tech #2:   Well, nothing, of course, but I was wondering—and you don't have to answer . . .

Tech #1:   Answer what?

Tech #2:   I was wondering if you have a name for them?

Tech #1:   A name for whom?

Tech #2:   You know who.

Tech #1:   Oh. I call them the Sleepers.

Tech #2:   And us, what are we then?

Tech #1:   Support staff.

■

So Ballerina Mouse keeps on trying, and the years go by in a shower of mockery from her fellow dancers, who are, without exception, younger than she is. At recitals it becomes her job to hand out programs and staff the punch table, and although Mme. Suzette keeps promising Ballerina Mouse she will be cast in the very next recital, it never seems to happen.

Then one day, after a particularly hard practice session after which her fellow dancers squirt her with the sticky liquid left in the bottoms of their energy drink cups, pretending they are helping her cool off, Ballerina Mouse leaves the studio but instead of going home, walks straight to a gun store, where . . .

*Stop it, Heather. Absolutely not.*

# XII

■

Episode One, *The Burrow*, Scene Two

HEATHER is alone in the kitchen. We watch her put groceries away, a process that involves opening and shutting the cabinet doors many times over. Clearly this is a young woman who struggles to find the right places for things. Finally, she sits down with an arrowroot cracker, strawberry jam, and a mug of Earl Grey tea.

**Heather:**      I don't know when it was I lost my nerve, exactly. Maybe it was going out on auditions at all hours of the night and day, every day of the week, including weekends, and, after each of them, hearing, "We'll call you," or "Hey, honey, I might have a part for you in the future, but meanwhile how'd you like to go out for a little drink." Or "Sorry, too tall," or "too short," or "too young," or "too thin." And lately I've been thinking I should get out of this weird place because, honestly, it's been forever since I saw the sun, but in point of fact, what good did the sun ever do me in the past? Anyway, no matter where I go, I'll need somewhere to live, and a job, too, so in the end I'd just have to come back here or somewhere like it, and get back on the phone again. Am I having a break-down? It's certainly possible, but how can I tell? I've never had one, so I don't know the signs, and that makes me anxious all by itself. I'm not stupid; I've read how things can slip away from people—I think it's happening to Madeline, too, though she'd never admit it—little by little and then, like swimmers, before they know it, they're too far out to get back to shore, back to the spot on the beach where they left their blanket that is so far away they can't even make it out. Help (softly). Help.

MADELINE walks in, wearing a blue bathrobe, pro-vocatively open, and, on seeing HEATHER, closes it.

**Madeline:**   Hey, honey. You don't look so great. How are you doing?

**Heather:**   I don't know. Maybe not so good, I think.

**Madeline:**   Gee, that's too bad. Do you want to talk about it? Me, I can hardly get any sleep these days. Something's keeping me up, I don't know what, but I don't suppose the same things that are bothering me are bothering you. Excuse me for interfering, but you're pretty; why don't you just get yourself a boyfriend? I know the pickings are pretty slim around here, except for Jeffery, that is. And as far as that goes . . . well, I don't know. I used to date him once, and there's something about him that's special in a way. If you don't snap him up I may well change my mind and take him back again myself.

MADELINE walks over to the refrigerator and looks in.

**Madeline:**   Say, do you mind if I do a little cooking while we talk? It calms me down, and maybe it will help you, too.

**Heather:**   You go right ahead.

**Madeline:** Hmm ... beets and hamburger [she smells it]—still good—and onions. What can I make from that?

**Heather:** I don't know.

**Madeline:** Wait! I'm thinking, maybe . . . red hamburger hash!

**Heather:** I've never heard of that.

**Madeline:** So let's you and I live dangerously. Let's see what happens.

She starts chopping up the onions and beets, and puts them in a frying pan with a little oil. HEATHER watches for a while, then loses interest.

**Heather:** Well, I've got to go. I'm expecting a phone call any minute.

**Madeline:** What? Oh, sure honey. Don't forget what I said about Jeffery. He's pretty special.

HEATHER leaves, MADELINE continues stirring. VIKTOR walks in and sniffs the air.

**Viktor:** Hey! Is that food I smell?

■

*I'm getting rich*, Viktor thinks, *but not quite rich enough just yet*. Still, a little rich anyway, and a person has to measure his life against something, so why not make it money? There's love, of course, but how can a person tell if he's ahead or behind in love? There's health and all that goes with it, but that's a one-way street, he knows; a person can hold back the water of that particular dam only so long, and then the water is going to win, is going to pour over the top, and if that person doesn't pick up his camping gear and get the hell out of there he'll be buried in a wall of mud. As for Madeline, well, she's okay enough, and sometimes she sings crazy stuff to him, which he likes, but—hello—when Viktor gets out of here he won't be taking her. Sorry, kid. Tough break.

Madeline is a survivor though, so Viktor's not worried about her. Really, the guy Viktor feels bad for is the Duck Man because he was the one who stole Madeline from the Duck Man. But when he lets her go, maybe Duck Man can get her back. Fair enough. And if she thinks Duck Man is so great, she can have him, Viktor thinks. And does Viktor care? Not much. The mystery, if there is one, is why she ever left Jeffery.

*I am such a pig.*
*I am such a pig.*
*I am such a pig.*

*I am such a pig,* Viktor says to himself.

And oddly it feels good to say this, like waving to himself from across the street, seeing a sort of familiar stranger, a mirror image, but one that reflects a truth that seems irrefutable, a truth that, once having been recognized, allows the recognizer some considerable latitude of behavior. *Yes, thank you, Viktor,* Viktor says. *You are right. You are such a pig. And happy as a pig in mud.*

■

Then Ballerina Mouse has an operation, one that's done by little mouse doctors and mouse nurses, who take tiny X-ray pictures and move things this way and that, and pretty soon they turn her foot around so it faces a different direction and everything is better. But of course then Ballerina Mouse has to start practicing with her newly redirected foot, learning everything over again, in part because she's had so much downtime, what with her stay in the hospital and all, but also because some of the muscles she's now using aren't used to working in that direction at all, but in fact the opposite one, so it's like starting from scratch.

And Ballerina Mouse does work hard—even harder than she did before, which was already indisputably hard—so bit by bit her old skills return and she learns new skills as well. She gets a small role, and then a larger one, and then a larger one, and, at last, she becomes a star.

*Well, no.*

*Who would believe that?*

■

Among insects—the Captain thinks—among fish, among rats, iguanas, reindeer, dogs, lions, and tigers, there are no celebrities, nor are there celebrities among orangutans, or chimps, or bonobos, or apes. No, among none of these is there a need to raise one of their own above the rest, except to lead, or breed, or teach. No raccoon will ever choose another raccoon and set it off as an object of desire and envy. No snake ever said: *I wish I could be you*, to another snake. No toad ever fantasized about being a toad different than itself.

So what is this desire, the Captain wonders, we humans have to live out an alternate story to our own lives? Is there an entirely different life out there for him, one he never lived or has still to live or a whole series of possible lives heading off into infinity, like seeing a mirror reflected in another mirror? He looks around. On one hand there is the coffeepot, the microwave, and, in the next room, the giant TV screen—himself reflected on the surfaces of each in a way—and on the other hand, there is the leather couch with its feet resting on little rubber cups so as to keep it from digging holes into the Persian carpet, the coffee table, and, lying on the table, the Walther, right where he left it after having given it a thorough cleaning. And there he is too, standing amid all of it, a celebrity. But what would his life be like if he were just an ordinary seaman?

■

Madeline thinks: Has anyone down here in the Burrow ever taken a minute to recognize how important cooking is? I mean, what else does a person do three times a day, every day? Not sex, that's for sure. But here, even with the limited facilities, it's still possible for a stong-minded person with a talent for combining odd ingredients to carve out a gracious meal from the groceries that come, more or less in the middle of the night, several times a week when no one's there to witness their arrival. Let's see—kale, eggs, and breadcrumbs. How about a kale omelet with cheese covered with golden breadcrumbs? That sounds good, I think I'll try it, but will my fellow renters even notice, or will they just take it for granted as they have so many, many other things? Will Viktor care? Jeffery? Even Raymond? Who am I kidding? And what about that twit Heather, who walks around in pretty much a daze, making faces to herself and jumping to one side whenever I pass her in the hall, like she's afraid I'll give her a smack? Honestly, I'm afraid the girl is headed for a breakdown, and I just hope I'm not around to see it when it comes; I have the feeling it could be messy.

I should charge people for my services, but then, if they said they didn't need them, the truth is that I'd be bored without cooking, so I'll just keep on doing what I do. *Iron Chef Madeline*. On-the-job training for some future career. No. Not just a career, but for being the queen of all celebrity chefs.

■

The fact is, Raymond's head *is* small for his body, a trait that Madeline used to poke fun at in the days when she and Jeffery were, as Jeffery used to say, "an item." Back then, the two of them would speculate on the man's strange affinity for ducks and Madeline would say, "I can't imagine any woman finding him attractive, can you?" then give Jeffery a little squeeze.

But toward the end of their relationship, just before she was about to leave Jeffery for Raymond, she once said, "You know, if you look at any of these decoys around Raymond's room, you'll see their heads are small too, at least compared to their bodies, and they are beautiful."

So Madeline, Jeffery tells himself, is now onto this string of two guys in a row: the first with a small head, and the second with overlarge hands. What does this say about her? Does Madeline have some kind of thing for freaks? And more important, is it possible there is something weird about him too that Madeline can see but he can't?

■

All right. Say Ballerina Mouse never has an operation on her foot because she can't afford it, and because nobody is willing to do something that takes so much skill gratis. Skill, after all, takes time and money to acquire. It *can't* be given away for free, and even if Ballerina Mouse could find just one benevolent and kind old mouse doctor who would agree to help her out, such a complicated operation takes not just *one* generous individual, but a whole team of other mouse doctors, and nurses, and anesthesiologists, to say nothing of the costs involved in keeping a hospital operating room up, running, and free from harmful bacteria, not even counting the whole time spent afterward on the recovery ward, post-op, dressings to be changed, meals in bed, vital signs, and later, still further down the line, all the time that's needed in the rehab facility. Don't forget to add that.

But then, just as the other mice are laughing at her once again for her so-called hopeless dreams, and just as she's about to call it quits, almost by accident she discovers tap dancing and it turns out she's a natural.

*Nope.*

■

*Twilight souls*, who neither exist nor do not exist, the Captain thinks, but who reside in a moment that is inseparable from memory, who live in hope that is a kind of hopelessness, a dream identical to their lives, whose lives pass but never change, are neither spoken nor unspoken, are only here, are only gone, are only able to look back and say: *There, that's where I was*, but never *where I will be*, never *where I am*. That is: caught in a place between a name and no name and without a future.

He can honestly say that he does not hate them, because he does not. But come on, when one of them—
those others, as he likes to think of them—is gone, will it
truly be missed? Can one ever be?

■

Madeline dreams she has her own cooking show, called
*Cooking with Madeline*, and in her dream, she's at the
television studio where the show is filmed, on a set
called "Madeline's Kitchen," the only set, in fact, for the
entire show. It's a place she loves because in Madeline's
Kitchen the plates are always clean, the utensils
sparkle, the knives are always sharp. In fact, it is this
same set in which all her dishes are prepared for the
television audience—several dishes, actually, each one
at a different point of completion, so as to create the
illusion of progress without having to pay a full crew to
stand around and wait.

And with her on the set today is her director, Herb,
whose name she jokes about and with whom she's slept
a few times just in order to have something on him in
case he gives her any trouble, because he's married to
someone named Loraine, or Lurine—something like
that—and he wouldn't want news of an affair to get out.

Her cameraman, Ned, is there, too. She's still deciding whether or not to sleep with Ned, the negatives being his bald head and his being overweight, while the positives are that he calls her Honeybunch, something her dad used to call her back before the cancer brought him down—six terrible months, each one worse than the last.

Today, or maybe tonight (because she's dreaming this), Madeline is wearing her no-nonsense full apron, the red one with pockets that people can order for themselves from cookingwithmadeline.com, and her hair is in a bun. Warm and classy is the vibe the show strives to project onto the viewing audience, and it succeeds.

"Ready?" Herb asks, but for some reason Madeline is nervous for the first time in years—surprising, actually, with her being a pro and all, knowing that through the magic of retakes it's impossible for her to fuck up.

"Ready?" Ned asks.

So today's show, of all things, is how to stuff a suckling pig, which they are filming ahead of time for the holidays, because the holidays are a time when things like killing babies, even baby cows, and pigs, and sheep, tend to seem okay as long as they are wrapped in the guise of tradition. "Hi, and welcome to *Cooking with Madeline*," says Madeline in that friendly tone that nonetheless suggests that people need to keep their distance, another trademark of her on-air persona. "Today's show isn't for the squeamish." She hates this phrase, and didn't want to use it at all until the network's legal team promised if she didn't she'd get her ass sued off. And then she walks over to the counter where the pig is waiting, but to her surprise: it's alive. Madeline looks at Herb. Is this the way things are supposed to be? He nods, Yes it is. Go ahead.

Madeline looks around for a butcher knife. Okay, she thinks, if that's what you want. But today, for the first time ever, there is no butcher's knife, or chef's knife, or even a paring or a fruit knife. There are no knives at all. There are vegetable peelers, a garlic press, a set of measuring spoons, metric and regular, a meat thermometer, a whisk, a stainless-steel shrimp deveiner, an apple corer, salt and pepper grinders, basting brushes, wooden spoons, spatulas, measuring cups, pasta scoops, fat skimmers, and an egg slicer, but no knives.

Again she looks at Herb, giving him a *what-happened-to-the-knives?* kind of look, but he just nods happily. *Go ahead*, he signals again. Madeline looks at Ned, but she can't see anything behind the camera except for one beefy shoulder, so there's no help from him at all. Forget sleeping with Ned, she thinks.

Too bad for him.

■

So then all the other mouse ballerinas laugh at Ballerina Mouse for even trying, because it's apparent to everybody she isn't making any progress at all, and that the ballet school, and especially the teacher, Mme. Suzette, is just taking her money. At last, even Mme. Suzette, who until then had been using Ballerina Mouse's tuition to make the payments on her car, a Toyota Corolla, pays the loan off, and finds herself embarrassed pretending there is any chance at all, no matter how slim, for Ballerina Mouse. The upshot is that Mme. Suzette takes Ballerina Mouse into her office after class one warm afternoon and, after telling her to sit down for a minute—during which time Ballerina Mouse thinks her mom has died or something—Mme. Suzette tells her that while she truly admires the stupendous effort Ballerina Mouse has put into this whole enterprise, Ballerina Mouse, in Mme. Suzette's opinion, would be pushing the borders of sanity if she continued trying to be a ballet star.

So the little mouse, her heart frankly broken, gives up and settles down to a sedentary life. She works in her garden from time to time, but mostly she watches television, and in the process gains a considerable amount of weight, making any reconsideration of her exit from the world of dance even more impossible, until one day, while watching a nature program about dolphins, there is a news flash in which the commentator announces that a terrible tragedy has taken place: the town's only ballet theater has caught fire right in the middle of a performance, and every single ballerina, from the most inexperienced to the star, including the beloved teacher, Mme. Suzette, has burned to death.

*No.*

■

Then in her dream Madeline says: *Okay. You want this; you'll get it.* After all, that's how she became a star, a celebrity, as opposed to all those other people in the world who without a doubt are better cooks than she, either as hobbyists or actual professionals who work in restaurants, but none of them ever got their own network celebrity cooking show, let alone a whole line of celebrity-endorsed products. Okay, she thinks—no knives—this will be one for the books, or at least for the Internet, and, grabbing the meat thermometer, she tries to guess where the squirming baby pig's heart must be. She knows that in humans it's slightly to the left of center, but honestly, she can't remember where it is in pigs, so she decides to aim for the middle and hopes that she'll get lucky. She brings the thermometer down hard, but whether the heart is to the left or the right turns out to be entirely unimportant because at the last minute the pig turns, and all she gets is something that results in a spray of blood coming out of its mouth together with the most god-awful noise, and the sound of its tiny hooves scraping the counter as it tries to get away—who can blame it?—but luckily she catches its back foot just in time and holds it even though it's nearly pulling her arm off, because don't let anyone ever tell you that a pig isn't strong even as a baby, and if this one were twenty pounds heavier there'd be no way at all that she could keep it on the countertop, but so far she's got it—she's got ahold of it even though it's moving so much she flat gives up on any possibility of aiming at anything at all, so she just starts stabbing. *Stab, stab, stab*, blood everywhere as out of a corner of her eye she sees Ned smile and give her a thumbs-up while, next to him, Herb's nodding like one of those goddamn wooden drinking birds her dad used to buy her at the State Fair when she was little, the kind you can hook

to the side of a glass or a cup and watch bob back and
forth, but it doesn't seem like this baby pig is even
tiring, and meanwhile, all the time she's doing this, a
part of her—out of self-protection, she guesses—is far
away, the place she sometimes goes when she's having
sex with Viktor—trees, a quiet stream, blue skies, green
grass—and certainly he (or is it a she-pig?) ought to be
tiring by now, what with the loss of blood and fluids
in general, these last mentioned spraying in every
direction at once, so she's glad that, on the one hand she
chose to wear this particular apron, but on the other she
also knows her dress is ruined on those parts the apron
doesn't cover, which are many, and her hair is coming
loose from its bun as well. Meanwhile, if anything, the
pig is getting stronger, more desperate, something that
she, *stab*, finds she can relate to, *stab*, even as it occurs to
her that her show, *Cooking with Madeline*, may well be
canceled because, even if this particular episode is never
aired, there's no way somebody, probably that bastard
Ned, is going to miss making a bundle on a pirate
video, so she keeps on stabbing even though her arm
is becoming tired, and thank God, she thinks, that she
still works out at the gym three times a week, triceps
and biceps, because otherwise that pig, *stab*, would be
long gone, *stab*, probably racing around the floor of

Madeline's Kitchen, leaving a trail of blood, of course, and what kind of a career will she be able to have after this whole sorry episode is viewed a few million times online?

Well, the fact is, "after that" will probably mean the late-night talk shows, though she doubts that they'll have her on as anything but an object of mockery to laugh at, *stab*, because the little bastard keeps on moving, *stab*, but maybe, *stab*, maybe, *stab*, this could be, *stab*, some kind of conversion moment, she thinks, still stabbing, her arm like the drinking bird itself, the same kind of moment she will later explain, *stab*—because people seem to like these moments—the kind, *stab*, that Saul—or was it Paul?—had on the road to Tarsus or, *stab*, maybe Damascus, *stab*—the Road to Nowhere for all she cares—but, *stab*, then she can do a TV spot for PETA, yes, *stab*—genius!—the kind where she explains how once—and the pig is *finally* slowing down—she was *so* wrong, she realizes this now, to have taken the life of a fellow traveler on our fragile planet Earth, particularly on a religious holiday, on television, where kids could see it, but now she's learned, *stab*, to be, *stab*, a better, kinder individual, *stab*, because in the long run, *stab*, what people want to hear, *stab*, is how things, *stab*, always turn out for the best, and later, when she does the PETA spot, she'll say she really really loves pigs more than anything, except maybe those cute kitties and puppies that you see for sale in so many pet-store windows during the holidays.

∎

The Second Council of the Lateran under Pope Innocent II in 1139 banned the use of crossbows against Christians. Today, however, the crossbow has a complicated status. While some jurisdictions treat crossbows as firearms, others do not require any sort of license at all to own a crossbow—even for felons. In yet other places, the crossbow is regarded as a useful substitute for firearms, much in the same way that methadone is prescribed for former heroin addicts.

∎

Or: Being an intelligent mouse, Ballerina Mouse comes home from practice one day, her ears still ringing from the falsely encouraging shouts from Mme. Suzette of "Beau travail," "Bon tour," and "Ne quittez pas." Sitting in a chair on her back porch, a glass of iced tea in her tiny paw, Ballerina Mouse starts for the very first time to assess the situation as best she can. *As hard as you try, which is very hard,* she thinks, *by no stretch of the imagination are you making the kind of progress you need to make to become a star.* Ballerina Mouse looks out at her backyard and sees the wading pool, and the sandbox, and the swing on the tree, barely moving in the breeze. The garden is wilting beneath the heat of summer, as are the azalea bushes. *You are nearly a grown mouse,* she tells herself. *It's time for you to learn to be flexible. It's time to give up this crazy dream you've had since you were a child of being a ballerina who just happens to have a hurt foot, and to try something else, something that will help others. You could go to medical school, for example,* Ballerina Mouse thinks.

So Ballerina Mouse applies to several medical schools and is actually admitted to two of them—not the best, but not the worst, either—choosing the less expensive of the two and finishing with honors. Then, after graduation, she turns down the possibility of a comfortable practice in favor of traveling all over the world to help poor mice who cannot afford primary care, and in the process she helps thousands. At last one day after several years of doing good for others, she decides, what the fuck: she's not getting any younger and, using the skill set she's acquired in all her years of practice, plus a few new ideas she has come up with herself, in a groundbreaking operation Ballerina Mouse operates on her own foot, without anesthesia. And although it's too late for her to go back to being a ballerina, in part because she's still packing several extra pounds from lack of regular ballet practice, this self-performed surgery, combined with her past history of indefatigable good deeds, earns her some big humanitarian award, like the Nobel Prize or something.

*No.*

■

"In my dream," Raymond is saying, "all I could see were the shapes of dancers dancing in a darkened room, so dark that faces couldn't be seen, only the forms of bodies, and even those were so uncertain in shape it was impossible to tell which were male, and which female."

■

"You know," Jeffery tells Raymond late one morning in the kitchen over a breakfast of cold cereal and juice, "I don't believe Louis is coming back."

# XIII

■

It's been a long day, what with one thing and another, but now at last it's bedtime, practically the Captain's favorite time of the day. His bed, king-size, and for himself alone, makes up for all those years at sea when—even as a captain—he had only a narrow bunk. Now here it is, silk sheets and his secret vice, a lavender-scented pillow for sweet dreams. There's also a CD player on the table next to the bed, ready to repeat his favorite disc, *La Mer*, of course, through the night. Blinds shut. Lights off and everything should be restful, but still the Captain can't get out of his mind what that young guy in the plaid shirt was shouting. Despite his best efforts he's transported back in time to the set of that stupid television show where he'd been asked to be a sort of celebrity technical advisor to some actor or another—who can keep actors straight?—playing the role of a captain who couldn't tell land from sea, or something like that. If only he had just said, "No, I'll pass," the whole nasty business might have been avoided.

To this day, why they needed him remains a mystery—he supposed that thanks to that pirate incident on the *Valhalla Queen* he was virtually the only captain they had ever heard of, or at least the only one with an agent. But why he had accepted the offer, against his better judgment, he did know: namely, the pay he got for the brief trip to Kansas, where the show was being filmed, was far more than he ever received for piloting even the largest ships. The trick, Paul, the director, had told him was that, while the captain character was meant to be authentic, he couldn't be so authentic that he made the commune members seem inauthentic. "Don't forget," Paul had said, "it's a comedy."

Maybe—but the truth is that the Captain found the whole episode, involving a washed-up member of his own profession, to have a sad and tragic undertone, even despite the presence of that cute actress, Heather Something. And because he knew from his experience at sea that it was important to keep these negative feelings from the crew lest they let the vessel of the show drift off its course and end up on the rocks, he'd kept things lively by making small jokes at the gentle expense of some touchy teenage wise-ass in the cast, jokes that Heather, in particular, had appreciated. In the end, however, it hadn't worked. Maybe the exact opposite, in fact.

Fortunately, no one else at the lecture seemed to notice anything was seriously wrong, and his bearded, plaid-shirted accuser had been shuffled off almost as soon as the man finished shouting his completely unfair and accusatory message.

The Captain thinks about writing a note to his hosts thanking them for the sturdy ushers of the Masonic Hall, but decides, in the end, that would only call attention to the whole ridiculous incident.

■

"Have you ever thought," Jeffery says to Raymond, "that we could be some kind of an experiment?"

They are hanging out in the kitchen, late, as usual. Raymond is drinking a diet cola. Jeffery is eating cheese balls and sipping coffee. "I mean," Jeffery says, "that we get practically free rent, the food arrives on time and we don't even have to ask. Plus the place is full of mirrors. Has it ever occurred to you that maybe those mirrors are there so people can watch us through them?"

Raymond looks into his can of soda. *What is he looking for?* Jeffery thinks.

"I never thought of that," Raymond says, raising the can and taking a sip. "But what kind of person would want to spend his life watching someone else's life? I don't think it's anyone either you or I would care to know."

■

The so-called trivial incident the madman (*Plaidman*, the Captain thinks) was referring to happened at the very end of the Captain's consultancy at *Mellow Valley*, at which time the more or less tragic implication of that episode's plot—the inability to sustain oneself through agriculture, and that, for all practical purposes, there was no real difference between being lost on land or at sea—had finally been revealed. They had finished shooting early for the day, and by that afternoon the Captain had had more than a few glasses of wine—out of boredom, he supposed. Then, after the teen (named Scooter? Junior?) stomped off to sulk over some mild remark the Captain had made, and the rest of the crew fell silent, the Captain got up from the table to find the wretched boy and coax him back.

Thus it was that the Captain found himself outside. Once there, however, and slightly confused by more glasses of wine than he was used to imbibing, plus a misleading series of "Off Limits" signs, he had turned a corner to see the actresses who played Judy and Heather (!) in a state of complete undress, sharing a communal moment in "the women's shower area," beneath a powerful stream of water that poured in a delicious torrent onto their shoulders, backs, and breasts, and descended to their pubic deltas—in Heather's case especially—in a drop that took him back to, of all things, his very first sight of Malabata Falls, a nearly inaccessible and barely known spot (except to a handful of travelers) that surely would have been one of the Wonders of the World if only it were more easily reached. And the spot was remarkable not only on account of its terrifying roar but also for the myriad colors of orchids and bromeliads, including rare hanging pineapple plants, their diamond patterns reflected in the crystal waters at the bottom of the falls like a necklace of many-colored jewels that, having momentarily become undone, eternally plunged between their owner's luscious breasts, surrounded (the falls, not the breasts) by the screech of wild monkeys and the squawks of brightly colored parrots, some of which had been trained by the cunning natives to swoop out of practically nowhere and snatch away bills of any denomination from such visitors careless enough to be counting them out of doors.

Yes, all this and more flooded back into the ocean that was the Captain's mind even as he stood, blending the sight of the one cataract with the other: the falls and the water cascading down the two beauties— especially Heather—rubbing and scrubbing the sweat of that final day's shoot from their bodies, seemingly oblivious to his presence until the very moment their shouts of "Help!" and "Pervert!" drew him back from his reverie, during which he had apparently forgotten he was still holding up to his eye the video camera he had brought along on his search for the overly sensitive, sulking teenager just in case he came upon some native wildlife—a snake or billy goat, to name but two examples—in the process.

And even worse, it turned out that in his ignorance of modern media technology he was not just *holding* the video camera, as he had thought, but in his excitement his finger must somehow have been pressed against RECORD the entire time, so that it might have easily appeared to those who came running at the girls' frantic cries—as indeed it would have to himself had he not been on the other end of the lens, so to speak— that the whole scene had been somehow premeditated by him instead of being merely the grotesque accident it was, an accident made even more ironic because until that moment the Captain's sole moral compass had been the Code of the Sea.

The result? More screaming. People running from everywhere. A headlock, a punch, a badly aimed kick or two, and then, shouts—"Get Him!" and "Captain Perv!"—followed by four days in the local jail and charges, later mercifully dropped.

And then, to make matters even worse, for some reason the show was canceled before the episode even got a chance *to air*.

■

## NOTE: CONCERNING THE APPAREL OF THE TECHNICAL STAFF

Actually the much-complained-about "special hat" referred to earlier is called a Phrygian cap and has a soft conical dome with the top pulled forward. It is associated in antiquity with the inhabitants of Phrygia, a region of central Anatolia thought by many to be the birthplace of Western civilization. In the western provinces of the Roman Empire this cap came to signify freedom and the pursuit of liberty, perhaps through confusion with the pileus, the felt cap of emancipated slaves of ancient Rome. Accordingly, the Phrygian cap is sometimes called a liberty cap; in artistic representations it signifies freedom and the pursuit of liberty.

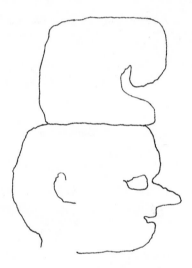

■

Oh, and the Captain forgot to mention: the sexual offender label was dropped on the condition that he be banned for his entire life from getting anywhere near the production set of any television show whatsoever, including nature programs.

■

In Raymond's dream there is a knock on the door of his room and, when he opens it, there is Louis, just standing there, wearing a blue cardigan sweater and still in his slippers. Louis looks sad, as if the sadness is coming not from anything that happened, but from deep inside. He shifts his weight from side to side.

"Come in," Raymond says. "Would you care to have a seat?"

Louis stays where he is, framed in the doorway, the dark hall behind him. "No thanks," he says. "I just came to say good-bye."

And before Raymond can answer, Louis turns and walks down the hall, in the direction of the Burrow's door, but when Raymond rushes after him there is no one there. He's simply gone, as if the hall has swallowed him.

■

Or: Ballerina Mouse wakes to realize in the end that she has only been dreaming, and she has no bad foot, nor does she have the slightest interest in being a ballerina. She can't imagine where that came from.

What she likes is cheese, and not much else, truth be told, because, after all, she's only a mouse.

*Definitely not.*

■

*Do I have any children in this world?* The Captain asks this question from time to time, not urgently, but more as speculation. Certainly, it's possible, maybe even likely, given the number of ports he's visited and the number of women with whom he has had intimate relations. But if he *did* have unaccounted-for children, a person would think that, sooner or later, one of them would have shown up at the front door of his mansion, being as he is a celebrity now, and easy to track down. "Hello," such a hypothetical boy would say. "My name is Captain Junior."

But how would such a boy find him?

And how could such a child afford the ticket?

Tennyson, former poet laureate of the British Empire, called the products of such unions "a dusty race," and deemed them superior to either parent considered separately.

The Captain takes serious issue with Lord Alfred in that regard, however. *Twilight souls* is what the Captain

calls them. And that name, Junior, brings back everything he had been trying to forget about that embarrassing scene at the shower. *That* was the kid's name, of
course.

Could he possibly have been the Plaidman?

Though that was years ago, and no one knows better
than he that people change.

■

The fact is that Madeline has been feeling a little down
lately. Well, *very* down. The Burrow was good enough
when she first arrived, a welcome respite from all the
ex-boyfriends and bill collectors of her former life, a
life that seems so distant now she can hardly remember
it, and she does appreciate the Burrow's privacy and
quiet, even though most nights recently, with the
sounds of machinery grinding somewhere outside the
Burrow's walls, the "quiet" part of that equation is gone.
Back when she first moved in, she was also happy to
have a whole set of new faces (now old ones) to look
at, and also the chance to do some cooking, maybe
develop a repertoire, as they say in the business, so she
could move on one day. But here she still is, and how
much serious cooking can anyone do in this dump of

a kitchen anyway, with an oven door that barely shuts, the temperature knob missing so that she has to use the cheap tin thermometer hanging from the baking rack, and even that keeps falling off every time she slides in a sheet of biscuits? Not to mention that she has to use the food provided, which at the start was fun, like a game, or being on one of those cooking shows where they hand you a piece of celery, a donut, and a clove of garlic, and you're supposed to create some fabulous new dish. But now it's just annoying, plus, one of the top burners in front of the stove's grease-spattered mirror (*whose idea was that?*) is totally dead, and if people think it's easy to cook for five people using only three burners, they have another thing coming. *What* thing, she's not sure.

Raymond used to have a thing about food being sadness, which, she noticed, never stopped him from packing the stuff away. Now, however, and for the first time, she wonders if he could possibly be right: Cook food. Pour food into oral cavity. Grind up with teeth. Down hatch. Wait for stomach to turn it into a brown-ish slush. Wait for good parts of slush to be sucked into blood. And finally, everything *not* good, *leftovers*, she calls them, exits the body in not the most pleasant way possible. If only there were fireworks every time we shit, or music came out, she thinks—something to make it more enjoyable—but mostly there isn't; the only person she's ever known who seems to thoroughly get into every part of the digestive process is Viktor. And then, there's the smell. Then, after all of that, what's left but to get ready for the next meal, and so on and so forth, until one day the whole process stops, and whatever that last meal was will just sit there, a little potluck to bring to the party of eternity.

She even finds herself missing Louis, whom she dated for a while, before he disappeared to wherever he went. One night he's there and then, for no apparent reason, the next night Louis is gone.

*What is happening to me?* Madeline asks. Maybe it's just that she's tired, and nothing else. Certainly that noise at night isn't helping her sleep, and though she knows she can stay in bed as long as she wants to in the morning because, well, there's nothing forcing her to get up, she's always been one to wake with the dawn.

Even though she can't see the dawn because she's in a burrow, which, practically by definition, means lacking windows.

Would a skylight help her feel better? Possibly. Madeline wonders if it would be such a big deal for her to just find someone to stick a not-so-fancy piece of glass in between her ceiling and the sunlight. *If I can get the landlord to agree,* Madeline thinks, *I might even pay for it myself.*

How expensive could it be?

And when was the last time she actually saw the landlord?

■

Episode One, *The Burrow*, Scene Three

VIKTOR and MADELINE are alone in the kitchen.

**Madeline:** Fancy meeting you here.

**Viktor:** It's not fancy at all. I just happen to be feeling hungry.

**Madeline:** When aren't you?

**Viktor:** Never.

**Madeline:** I can never figure out how you can burn up so much energy when you spend all your time just sitting in front of a computer screen watching stock prices go up and down, with only an occasional break for a little love.

**Viktor:**    Hey, don't underestimate yourself. You're *a lot* of love.

**Madeline:**    Which actually brings me to something: Why don't you ever take me anywhere?

**Viktor:**    Where exactly would you like to go?

**Madeline:**    I don't know. Anywhere. I can't remember the last time I was even out of here. Don't you ever get tired of making money? Don't answer that.

**Viktor:**    Well, I know one thing I don't get tired of.

**Madeline:**    [flattered, despite herself] Really.

**Viktor:**    Your tandoori chicken. I don't know how you do it, but it's delicious, particularly when you serve it with that aromatic rice of yours and the cucumber and yogurt thing. Maybe in your next life you should be an Indian. Didn't I see some fresh chicken in the refrigerator?

**Madeline:**    You did, but the chicken's the easy part. You can't make tandoori chicken without a jar of tandoori sauce, and I'm thinking that may be a little hard to come by. I don't even know how we happened to have the last one. It must have been left behind by somebody. Maybe it was Louis's.

MADELINE opens one cabinet after another without finding any sauce.

**Madeline:**   You can't say I didn't try.
**Viktor:**    Are you sure you looked everywhere?

As she opens the last door, what does she see but a jar of tandoori sauce!

**Madeline:**   Wow, a whole jar! We *do* have it.
**Viktor:**    I guess it's my lucky day.

■

Mornings are always the best for the Captain. There are the silences, the coffee, the fresh pastry (just one a day—he has to watch his waistline, grown a little since those calorie-burning days of pitching and yawing at sea). Also, there's the special quality of eastern light, so like the light far out in the ocean where the salt spray tempers and refracts the fleshy tones of, well, flesh, but with none of the troubling grays of twilight. At twilight this evening, he's scheduled for a talk in which he'll use the mutiny story once again, always a hit— at least so far. But the last time he used it, he spotted a young couple making out in the back of the room, paying no attention at all to his words. Could that have been the beginning of the end, the hairline crack in the hull that will wind up sinking the whole vessel of his lecture career? And suppose that ridiculous guy shows up, the Plaidman who brought up the *Mellow Valley* thing. If the Captain spots him early on, he can have him ejected, maybe have him roughed up a little, but if he shows up again at the end, during the Q & A, and starts repeating the same things, sooner or later people are going to start asking questions.

The Captain walks to the front window to look at the lawn and see how it's fared after the mysterious-hole incident. The sight of the lawn usually calms him down, but not today, because it's back—the hole—and exactly where it was before, so for a second he thinks maybe the patch job didn't work; that everything just dropped straight down again, but then he sees a ring of dirt around the edge, just like the first one.

He takes his cup and walks outside, though clearly at this point there is nothing new to see: just dirt and what might be the print of a shoe. The air is still cool. He'll call up his gardener again and tell him: "We'll just have to do better the next time." Maybe have him dump a shitload of poison down the hole, stuff it with a

few sacks of ready-mix cement, hose it down so it gets
good and hard, and then replant the top. That should
do it.

He walks back inside and calls the man, who says
he'll be over as soon as he gets his pickup out of the shop.
What's wrong with vehicles these days, the Captain
wonders, that they always need repair? It occurs to him
he ought to inquire of someone whether this holes-in-
people's-front-lawns business is a citywide phenom-
enon, or if it's directed specifically at him. He's made
a lot of enemies along the way—who hasn't?—but this
seems a strange and unnecessarily complicated way to
get revenge. Could the guy in the beard and lumberjack
shirt—Plaidman—be behind this attack on his lawn?
And if so, why?

■

Meanwhile, all over town, grass, flowers, weeds,
nameless trees are pushing their way up through the
soil, into the light and the air, into something they have
no name for.

■

On the other hand, if he just calls the police and asks them to investigate what the fuck is happening to his grass, sooner or later word is going to leak out to the press, who, for reasons of their own, will probably see it only as one in a long line of cheap publicity stunts. The Captain can picture the headline: "Aging Windbag Claims Mysterious Lawn Cavity." And then, before the ink is even dry on that morning's paper, everybody will be at the edge of his lawn—or on the lawn itself, for that matter—to take a look. And when they're done, they'll leave behind their soda cans and potato chip bags, gum wrappers, and those tiny plastic boxes breath mints come in. What is it with this modern obsession with the smell of your own breath, anyway? Many a time he has seen a complete stranger hold a hand out in front of his face and breathe into it. Never once, in all his years at sea, did he ever observe a sailor doing such a thing. And the result—his house, the one thing he loves these days, will become a sideshow. That would be all he needs, and, at the very least, he'd have to hire a security guard, which wouldn't come cheap. Or even worse, expense-wise, he might have to raise the wall around the place. Neither of these prospects makes him happy.

And so, like an unsteady midshipman climbing to the top of a swaying tall mast having been sent up there

by the first mate on some made-up errand that is supposed to initiate him into the unstinting demands of a
seafaring life, the Captain can feel his Death Quotient
rising.

■

Episode One, *The Burrow*, Scene Four

JEFFERY and VIKTOR are sitting at the kitchen table. It is late at night.

| | |
|---|---|
| **Jeffery:** | Viktor, I'm going to make myself another bagel. You want one? |
| **Viktor:** | What kind of bagels did we get this week? |
| **Jeffery:** | Onion and sesame. |
| **Viktor:** | That's all? |
| **Jeffery:** | That's it. If you want something else, I guess you'll have to go out and get it. Do you want cream cheese? |
| **Viktor:** | I'll take an onion with cream cheese. |

JEFFERY gets up, cuts two bagels in half, and puts
them in the toaster oven.

| | |
|---|---|
| **Jeffery:** | Listen, I have a question, and it may sound a little odd. |
| **Viktor:** | Shoot. |
| **Jeffery:** | How long has it been since you've been out? |
| **Viktor:** | What do you mean, "out"? I have investments to keep track of. I can't be going in and out every time I want a breath of fresh air. I could lose real money here. |
| **Jeffery:** | No, I don't mean that. I mean when was the last time you were even outside the Burrow? |
| **Viktor:** | I don't know. A couple of weeks ago. Maybe more. Maybe a couple of months. [pauses] Actually, if you want to know the truth, I can't remember. |
| **Jeffery:** | You find that odd? |
| **Viktor:** | Not particularly. I never thought about it. |
| **Jeffery:** | Neither had I, because I've been really busy working on this screenplay I'm writing. But then I got to thinking: *Jeffery, when was the last time you were out of doors?* |
| **Viktor:** | You call yourself by your own name when you talk to yourself? |
| **Jeffery:** | Of course. What else would I call me? |

**Viktor:**    You must have been talking to Madeline; she talks to herself sometimes, too. So what did you answer? When was the last time you were out?

**Jeffery:**   I couldn't remember.

**Viktor:**    And this proves?

**Jeffery:**   So I said to myself, "Well, you should make it a point to go out right now, right this second, not that you need anything, because everything we need is here, but, you know, just to do it."

**Viktor:**    And?

**Jeffery:**   And do you know what? Right then I started to make a list of all the times I'd tried to go outside before, including the last time, when I was about to leave and was standing right at the door and Raymond stopped me. Then, by the time I finished the list, it was too late. I never did go out.

**Viktor:**    The Duck Man! A nutcase, in my opinion. And anyway, I don't see what's so wrong with a person staying here and working. Maybe that screenplay will make you rich. Then you'll be glad you didn't waste your

> time walking around in the fresh air and
> leaves and stuff. You can get that anytime.

**Jeffery:** Maybe, but after that, I tried to leave again,
and then I got sidetracked again, and the
same thing happened after that, and after
that. So it's been a week now, and for one
reason or another I still haven't been outside. It's like . . .

The bell of the toaster oven rings. The bagels are ready.
JEFFERY takes them out and spreads cream cheese on
each. He gives one to VIKTOR.

**Viktor:** Come on—think about it. What is going
on outside that's so important anyway?
You can watch the news, can't you?

**Jeffery:** That's exactly what I told myself. But
lately I've been thinking, what if I'm under some kind of a spell, or secret power?
And then I tried to remember if anybody
here has mentioned being outside lately,
and I couldn't think of anyone who has.
So sitting here, right now, I just made my
mind up to start asking other people. You
know, you, obviously, and Heather, and

                 Madeline, and maybe even Raymond, al-
though I'm pretty sure what his answer
will be because he's happy just to stay in
his room carving decoys, and as long as
chunks of wood keep arriving from wherever, he's happy.

**Viktor:**       That's the Duck Man, all right.

**Jeffery:**       But doesn't that strike you as odd?

**Viktor:**       That he likes ducks? You should hear what
Madeline has to say on that subject.

**Jeffery:**       No, I mean where do those chunks of
wood come from?

**Viktor:**       I don't know. I guess somebody . . . or
maybe not. Maybe. Listen, I have to go.

**Jeffery:**       But wait. There's one more thing. Have
you ever heard of the Witness Protection
Program?

**Viktor:**       The federal one? Of course I have, but
what does that have to do with anything?
Now, I'll just take my bagel back to my
room and get to work. Have a good night.

**Jeffery:**       Thanks. You too.

JEFFERY is left alone in the kitchen, holding his bagel.

■

So instead of chewing over the story of the mutiny once again, maybe the Captain should tell his audience about the day he shot the rope that was holding the beautiful young native girl those devils from another tribe were taking away to be a hostage, or worse. The girl—what was her name?—Rima? Kojima? Bulima? She couldn't have been more than fourteen, but was already surprisingly well-developed. Also she was remarkably calm, seeing as how she was being led away to nearly certain death by vicious members of a rival clan. For a while he was sure that they must have drugged her, but then, once he had severed her rope tether with a single shot from the Walther, she took off like a rabbit until she got to the grassy edge of the river, dived in, and climbed on board the ship, while the whole time the Captain covered her escape with a deadly accurate volley of bullets he kept firing into the bushes from the moving deck. And then, talk about a twilight individual finding surprising ways to show her gratitude! On second thought, it's probably not such a good idea to bring this up in public, chiefly because of the issues of a statutory nature, but also he doesn't want to make it seem as if he is gloating. *Those were the days,* he thinks, but since then what does he have to show for himself?

*Other than a series of fish-related endorsements and some lectures, not all that much,* if he's being honest.

■

Ballerina Mouse is dead, her head caught in one of those traps where the metal bar descends to snap a poor mouse's spine so rapidly the creature caught beneath, if it's lucky, dies instantly. If not, it gets caught by a part of a leg, or even its nose, or somewhere else, and has to suffer for as long as it takes to be found, or it finally and agonizingly dies. But Ballerina Mouse *was* lucky, because in that split second, the pain of her foot, the humiliation of her ballet lessons, the mendacity of Mme. Suzette, all of it, became only the extrusions of one final flush of consciousness, already forgotten, gone into the air, the flowers, the grass, the trees.

*No.*

■

To the *St. Nils Eagle*

Dear Editors,

Awhile ago I announced in the pages of your paper the formation of my organization (FQO.org) dedicated to the distribution of crossbows to needy servicemen and women, and since then I have received exactly zero donations. Far from being discouraged over a lack of public generosity, I am forced to conclude this is the case because practically no one reads what you write. (In point of fact, I myself have *never* seen anyone actually reading the *Eagle* besides myself.) For this, and other reasons relating to my present cash flow, I am now officially canceling my subscription.

Do not mistake this for a "cry for help" because it is not. I am fine, and if anyone needs help it would be those individuals who continue to publish a paper no one reads. Meanwhile, keep those crossbows coming.

Sincerely,
A Former (and for all I know, your only) Subscriber

■

*Tocar*: to touch.

XIV

■

Suppose a person is a genius, Junior wonders, maybe so far in front of other people that he never sees anyone, or speaks to anyone, or has any dealings with anyone, so for him, the petty needs and wants of others do not even exist, then how is that different from being dead? And even if this individual in question speaks with people once in a while—when he is in a store and has to ask where the bathroom is, for example—for those other parts of time when he's not speaking to anyone, is that the same as being dead? Or if two people live far apart and never say anything to each other, is that the same as each of them being dead?

Anyway, where did this thought come from? Does this have something to do with his father? Sadly, he can't quite work out that answer.

Or, Junior thinks, if a person is a genius, and surrounded by others who are also geniuses, maybe a think tank or something, and they all speak to each other, and see each other frequently, practically on a daily basis, and share their experiences with each other, how can they be sure they are geniuses?

To answer such a question, Junior would need to be a philosopher.

But Junior is not a philosopher. Not in the least.

Junior is a psychopath, and he is confusing himself with all these questions, one after another.

Roy is a good name, Junior thinks. He would like to have been called Roy.

But no, he had to get Junior.

■

Living here in the Burrow, what does Heather miss? Sunsets, kittens, grass, having a friend she can tell her secrets to. Feeling special.

What does Jeffery miss? Waterfalls, wind, spending money on things he doesn't need but feels like buying.

What does Viktor miss? Mud, seeing the sun go down, lying in warm mud.

What does Raymond miss? That's easy: ducks, geese, and coleslaw, which for some reason they never get in the Burrow because, Madeline says, no one ever leaves cabbage.

Madeline misses flowers, the sound of the ocean, the ability to go to a store and pick out her own groceries. Also a good stove would be nice.

What did Louis miss?

No one will ever know; he may as well be dead.

■

*Instinct.* That was what Dr. Barry Schwartz, her mentor in the Professional Practices Program, told her to heed. "Picture it, Tammy," Dr. Schwartz had said, "there you are in your rented office, no one else around, the security guard—if you are lucky enough to have one, which I doubt you will be—is either down the hall or out for coffee, and you are alone with a man, a patient, but still a man who is telling you his innermost secrets, ones he's fought to keep inside for years, and now you are prying them out of him bit by painful bit, coming closer and closer to his most guarded treasure, the secret of all secrets. Think about it: as you approach, his heart rate increases, his blood pressure rises, the identical physiological signs that would have exhibited themselves in his primitive past when he was hunting a deer or planning to carry a woman off to some glade for sex. So this man is stimulated; he's confused; he looks around. What does he see? A lovely, vulnerable attractive woman like yourself, my dear, the kind he has always desired, maybe even preyed upon at some time or other in the past because, after all, he's crazy, and now you are alone with him—just as the two of us are at this moment—in your rented office or maybe a spare room of your house, the use of which you are deducting from your taxes, and your legs are crossed, and your hair smells good, like strawberries, maybe a hint of clover too, and there is nothing between him and you but a yellow legal pad and the fat, expensive rollerball such as the one you are holding between your fingers now to scribble your notes.

"Instinct," Dr. Barry Schwartz repeated, breathing heavily. He touched the rim of his small, dark, Tyrolean hat, which for some reason or another in all the time she had known him she had never even once seen him remove from his head. Then he shut his eyes, reached up to his hatband, where he found a small, colorful duck feather, and he rubbed his index finger lightly over the feather's top.

He opened his eyes again. "Instinct, Tammy, is your only weapon, and, yes, you *are* a therapist and are there to help this man. Yet, on the other hand, it's not a co-incidence that many individuals who need help are also dangerous, and now *something* (your instinct) is telling you to get out of your chair. So do it! Make up some ridiculous excuse, such as you have to use the bathroom or check your parking meter, and, once you are out of his sight, run, run, run to your car and lock the doors. Then, take your cell phone and call 911, because though the person waiting for you in your office, with its cheerful curtains and Persian or Turkish carpet, the person currently checking the clock given to you by a major pharmaceutical company to see how long you've been gone, *is* needy, *very* needy, and in pain, *tremendously* in pain, and although your professional obligation is to return and help him, your instinct is correct: he is a monster and you should flee."

Dr. Barry Schwartz picked up his favorite pipe, a meerschaum carved in the image of Sigmund Freud, from where it had been lying on the desk and sucked in hard, very hard, even though it was currently empty of tobacco. A filthy habit, Tammy thought back then, and one she still abhors.

And what does any of this have to do with Junior's visit?

■

Tendrils, growing things, reaching out of the soil into what? And for what reason other than to grow?

■

Not that Jeffery's future television show, which will be called *The Burrow*, is the only seed in his creative garden. He's also thinking about a children's book, or maybe a screenplay for a children's movie, though he should probably work on the book first, then the movie after that to cash in on the success of the book, which will be called *Speedy Jack*. It will be about a dog named Jack whose back legs are cut off in an accident and who is fitted with a new kind of canine prosthesis made out of old automobile leaf springs, so that while wearing his new rear legs, Jack can jump even higher than before, and run a lot faster, too.

So the book will start, naturally enough, with Jack as a happy young dog. Then comes the story of the accident and, after that, how Jack practices with his new legs until he becomes super comfortable wearing them, first having races with other dogs and winning, then going on to racing deer and antelope, and beating them all until one day his owner takes him to Africa, where Jack races a cheetah, the fastest animal on earth, and

Jack winds up winning, seizing the title of fastest animal, at least for the duration of his life, from the disappointed cat. Finally, in the end, Jack will actually turn to face his readers and explain how grateful he is to have had the accident in the first place, because without it, none of his other adventures would ever have happened. In other words, Jeffery's book will teach children in a subtle way that sometimes life throws people curves, but with hard work and a positive attitude, even a bad situation can be turned around.

It's a narrative, Jeffery thinks, that will write itself once he can figure out one thing: what kind of accident will set Jack's story in motion. He'd like to have Jack trying to save someone, but at this very moment it's hard to imagine how that would work, exactly, when it's his rear legs, not the front ones, that will have to be cut off. *How do you lose your rear legs unless you are running away?* Also, if Jack had only *tried* to save someone and failed, there would be a dead person somewhere, and that could be a problem for children. Plus, there's the fact that no matter if someone was or wasn't saved, there's an accident, which means there's bound to be a lot of blood, and some parents might object, even though Jeffery plans to have Jack's owner standing by, watching the whole thing, and because his owner is a doctor he'll know exactly what to do to keep the bleeding to a minimum—probably tourniquets or something—followed by a rapid operation.

The doctor part makes sense because it will also explain how Jack gets to have a special prosthesis made, while most dogs that have their back legs cut off, whether in the process of saving someone's life or not, just die. So in the book it will be clear this isn't a normal event, but is made possible because the doctor knows the perfect person to call who can make Jack a new set of legs, so children will also learn how important it is to know the right people as they go through life, and *this* person, the prosthesis maker—though he will almost certainly lose money on the deal—makes a pair of them for Jack because he hopes for a ton of referrals from the doctor in the future. In addition, the prosthesis maker decides that the publicity that will come from Jack being a celebrity can only help his business with other doctors as well. In this way the children will learn there's usually a quid pro quo to most things in life.

*So it's never too late,* Jeffery thinks. The only problem is that original accident. Now what could it possibly be?

■

## TRANSCRIPT OF CONVERSATION FROM THE TECHNICAL STAFF

**Tech #1:**   How much do they know?

**Tech #2:**   Just enough, no more. They're not kept in the dark, exactly, but in a kind of twilight sleep, essentially the same as for a colonoscopy, or when they operate to remove certain growths—not quite awake, but still believing they are here—in a place, wherever that is—in their minds that has not gone away.

**Tech #1:**   And do you ever weep for them?

**Tech #2:**   Are you kidding? Would you weep for a small bird caught in a storm?

**Tech #1:**   And are there a lot of them out there?

**Tech #2:**   A whole lot, and not just the ones that you and I are in charge of, but all the rest being taken care of by other staff like us.

**Tech #1:**   Oh. So what's it like outside right now—can you tell?

**Tech #2:**   It's getting dark. Not dark yet, but heading there.

■

Has Viktor ever attempted to act like something other than a pig? Well, of course he has—who wouldn't? It's not as if he hasn't tried other animal behavior—something more expansive—a horse's, for example, or a lemur's, smaller but cute.

To illustrate just one occasion: Once in the seventh grade, he offered his lunch to a girl who'd left hers at home and so she arrived at school with nothing to eat. She was a pretty girl with long blond hair, so it's true that there may have been self-gratifying motives at work in Viktor's mind, but then, after she accepted his offer, she just got up from where she was sitting, the place where Viktor had sat down next to her, and walked to a spot two tables away and unpacked *Viktor's* lunch, enjoying one after another of *his* favorite foods, including a fudge brownie, an item his mother never ever put in his lunch before and, had he known it would be there, he most certainly would *never* have shared. Viktor just went hungry.

And there were other times also, in high school and after, but in the end Viktor has settled on this piece of homemade wisdom: *If you can't love the one you ought to be, love the one you are.* Which is, he knows, a pathetic kind of wisdom, but, hey, it's all he has. So Viktor tells himself, *Pigs are pigs, at least. And pigs tend to get very, very rich.*

Suppose he just moved into Louis's room without asking? Nobody would stop him. Louis isn't coming back. He's sure of that.

■

Still, the Captain has one more card to play—his hole card, no pun intended. If his career as a public speaker ever ends due to scandal or general lack of interest, he can always write a book and get rich. He vaguely remembers that one of the vessels he commanded (and there were a lot of them) had a cat as a mascot, until one day the Captain found it sleeping in a drawer in his cabin, getting its hair all over his neatly rolled socks, and so he took it straight out to the deck and tossed it overboard.

*I could write a story about a ship's cat*, he thinks, something warmhearted and aimed at children. Plus, there are advantages to writing a children's book. First, anyone can write one; second, there are hardly any words, hence fewer chances of making a mistake; third, kids' books are naturals for sequels; and fourth—and best of all—such books tend to be overpriced. In addition, very few of them hold up under spilled sugary drinks and sticky fingers, so they have to be rebought every time another generation comes around.

That's settled then. He's decided the cat should be orange and white, and have a ribbon around its neck. Also there can be battles with rats aboard the ship, but what will he call the cat in his book? Thor? Brutus? Spike? Nope. The actual cat he remembers tossing overboard must have had a name, but he never knew it. So for his book, how about something nonthreatening, a name children can instantly identify with? For example, a simple, harmless name—like Junior.

■

*You keep going forward, girl. Be Positive.* These are some of the signs Heather has put up to cover practically every square inch of her room, so, literally, there's nowhere she can look and not see them helping her. These are the messages that the Good Heather has left behind to aid the Not-Good-Enough Heather when that second one forgets, or gets discouraged, or even wants to sometimes . . . well . . . to make everything go away once and for all.

*Tomorrow is the first day of the rest of your life*, she read somewhere. Now it's pasted to her coffee table, and it is true; that's what tomorrow is, she thinks, but if that's true, what does that make today? But then, even without her trying, she can hear coming though the mostly instrumental music of the Easy Listening station she keeps on 24/7 another, harsher voice that says: "Heather, you've been saying that stupid line about tomorrow for a long, long time, and what has it ever done for you?"

Nonetheless, the Good Heather keeps patiently putting out these notes for the Not-Good-Enough Heather to read, hoping she'll learn from them, taping them onto the walls, pinning them to the cushions of the furniture, basically covering every flat surface, including the floor of the bathroom so the Not-Good-Enough Heather has something to read and inspire her while she is doing her business, but still, the Not-Good-Enough Heather doesn't appear to be getting the message. That Not-Good-Enough Heather, well, she's persistent. *No can do* is that Heather's mantra. Does Not-Good-Enough Heather even know the word *mantra*? And it's not as if that Heather-In-Between is getting any help from anyone else. Like once, when the Good Heather stuck a sign to the refrigerator in the kitchen of the Burrow—though of course she didn't tell anyone that she put it there—two days later somebody had changed *You can do it* to *You can't do it*, writing in the apostrophe and the *t* in purple Magic Marker.

Then, after looking at it for a few days, waiting for someone to change it back or say "I'm sorry," Heather-In-Between just took it down. But it was scary, as if some unseen hand knew better than she did what she'd suspected all along.

Still, writing these notes, even if they are just to herself, feels good, like progress is being made. After all, it's not impossible that one day the Not-Good-Enough Heather will read one, and suddenly a light will come on. "Oh," the Not-Good-Enough Heather will say, "I get it," and then she'll just disappear forever. Poof. Which is the reason that even while Heather is on the phone with some sex client—practically always, by the way—she wears her headset so she can have a hand free to write yet more notes: *That which doesn't kill me*, "Ooh, you know what I would like right now," *makes me*, "it's your big hard," *stronger*, "dick, and I'm not wearing any" *Slow and steady*, "underwear," *wins the day*, "so you can," *No*, "give it" *pain* "to me," *without*, "fast," *gain*. "Oh my God, that was so wonderful."

When was the last time she was really happy? It scares Heather how long ago it was. Maybe that time in high school, at the end of the Drama Club's production of *Oklahoma!*, in which she sang "I'm just a girl who can't say no," and everyone told her she had a big career ahead of her, and for about a half second, she thought she had. So from there to here, to this dark room full of scraps of paper—*You deserve the best*—how did that happen?

Unfortunately, that's not so hard to answer: practically straight from that production of *Oklahoma!* she went to the big city (well, a larger city), where she met Mr. Winkler, her agent, who promised he would protect her, and for a while, he did. She got a job at an auto show, and another at a county fair, and then, what was supposed to be her big break: a film shot on an island—the Island from Hell, she calls it now, and if only she had told them *no* when they kept refilling her glass of punch. But of course, she hadn't, so now there is the video—*the* video—reproduced so many times she can never, ever get it off the web or out of certain stores, like a target on her chest for all those guys who walk up to her at parties and on the street to smirk, "Hey, don't I know you from somewhere?" And needless to say—damn Winkler!—she gets zero in the way of royalties.

*A new start*, Heather thinks, *is what I need*, but if she leaves the Burrow, how is she going to afford it?

The sad thing is that she is demonstrably quite pretty, or at least, she used to be.

Spilt milk, Heather, her mother used to say, can never be put back into the glass again. Except with a sponge.

■

Also, Jeffery thinks, the story of Jack would be perfect for a kid's cartoon show, maybe with endorsements for dog food and pet supplies, meaning a lot more in terms of the income stream it will generate.

■

*Going.*

■

Junior goes into the closet in his bedroom and pulls out the special case in which he keeps his crossbow. *Old Stag Killer*, he says out loud, under his breath. *My old friend. My only friend.*

■

*Going.*

■

Though Raymond has ceased to mention it to Jeffery, that nightmare of him being a duck and dropping down in search of a pond has been returning—three times last week, and so far in this one it's up to four.

■

*And going even farther.*

XV

■

These days, when the Captain thinks about that incident on the set of *Mellow Valley*, he wonders if things were as verifiable as they appeared at the time or if they were part of a gigantic plot conceived and carried out by his enemies, members of some vengeful intelligence service from across the world, or possibly even one from his own country. He can think of several candidates who might have created that particular scenario, and the evidence is plentiful: sure, there was the business with the women taking showers and all, but someone *must* have moved the signs to get him lost. It only made sense that no one would admit to it. So that was one clue. And after all, he had made a bundle of enemies during those years of sailing in and out of ports. Because in point of fact, it would have been strange if a representative from one intelligence agency or another had *not* contacted him to ask if he would lend a hand in tipping the balance of the Cold

War this way or that. Well, they *had* asked, with gifts included, and naturally he had agreed to help them all.

Thus it was during those years the Captain sailed here and there, gathering intelligence like a patient honeybee, selling a little here, a little more there, until one day he stumbled across a piece of information (many important pieces, actually) that numerous people in several different governments would be most unhappy to have revealed. So of course it was necessary to discredit him. And, now that the Captain thinks about it, why *had* those producers of *Mellow Valley* contacted him in the first place, out of the blue like that? Sure, he was a celebrity, but there were plenty of other captains who could have done that job for less. Also, come to think of it, once he arrived at the set, his work was fairly minimal—a couple of questions about tying knots, something about a ship's log—but really his duties seemed only afterthoughts, a sort of cover to keep him busy and not too curious (all this, of course, in hindsight). In other words, the whole scenario leading up to the business with those women in the shower had been a deliberate setup to put him on the sidelines and keep him quiet just in case he ever decided to have a little chat with the reporters for the *St. Nils Eagle.*

Well, their scheme didn't work, did it? Or maybe it *did*, the Captain thinks, because he *has* kept quiet—until now, anyway, settled down as he is, far from the corridors of power, though still making a living, and a good one, as a celebrity in his own right. No threat, they probably think; their mission has been accomplished. But has it? He still knows plenty of people who would be very interested to hear what he has to say about certain things.

And then the hole suddenly appeared in his front lawn. Was it another warning, just to let him know they know where to find him? That he is vulnerable? Was it a reminder to keep quiet? How naïve do they think he is? First there was the incident in the shower, and now, not only is that being brought up again, but also there is the hole. Is he supposed to think it's only a coincidence? For that matter, could the hole in his lawn have been used for spying? Wasn't, come to think of it, a Myrmidon just another name for an inhabitant of Murmansk? Did his subconscious give him the clue he needed on the very first morning the hole appeared and he was too slow to process it? All this time he has assumed he was dealing with the CIA, but what if he is wrong? What if it was the work of the damned Ruskies? And if it was, what is *their* agenda?

Once the Captain settled on land he'd hoped never to have to use the Walther again, but who was it who said that in order to make a decent omelet first a person has to break a few eggs? The Ruskie, Lenin, that's who. And right now, depending on who or what is excavating his lawn, it is just possible that an Easter Egg Hunt is around the corner.

He can feel his Death Quotient going straight up, along with his blood pressure.

■

Episode One, *The Burrow*, Scene Five

JEFFERY is up late at night, standing alone in a corner of the kitchen.

**Jeffery:**     What is it with this constant grinding, 24/7, day and night, but particularly at night, when there are no other distractions to keep me from hearing it, forcing me to make it the virtual center of my brain? And, what's worse, although the noise may only be in my imagination, it seems that, like those annoying television commercials that appear at double the volume in the middle of whatever PBS special or wildlife program I might be watching, the noise of drilling—if that's what it is— actually increases during the night, almost as if, during the daytime, the noise-dampers, or mufflers, whatever things they use to quiet the machinery, are all in use, but at night, when the federal or state or local inspectors—whoever—go back home to cozy evenings around their flat-screen televisions with their families, all hell breaks loose and the giant teeth chew through the earth like so many enormous worms, creating their tunnels to who-knows-where— maybe Hades itself for all I know—louder, louder, louder—so whenever I try to write another scene for the very screenplay that, ironically, is supposed make me rich and free me from the tyranny of the din of such distractions, I can't think of the actual words I'm supposed to be using. I can't think about my characters; I can't think about anything remotely resembling a plot line; all I can think of is that noise, and

there's nothing I can do about it: I stuff
my ears with cotton, with wax, with waxed
cotton, rubber plugs, lumps of silicone—
nothing works—and meanwhile here I am,
a nervous wreck, unable to form a single
thought that is not centered around the
maw of that infernal machinery, not a single idea, not the slightest bit of whimsy or
touch of heartbreak that does not include
the grinding of those awful teeth, the howl
of metal against rock, the crunch of metal
pulverizing rock and everything else that
stands in its way. Oh Christ, Christ, if it
would only end.

Enter MADELINE.

**Madeline:**    Oh, hello Jeffery. What are you doing up
at this hour?

**Jeffery:**    Don't ask.

**Madeline:**    I was just about to make myself a toasted cheese sandwich with a little paprika
sprinkled on the top. Would you like me
to make one for you? I'm using the good
cheddar, of course.

**Jeffery:**     Yes, thank you.

JEFFERY watches as MADELINE slices the bread, lays the cheese on top, and sprinkles the whole surface with paprika.

**Madeline:**    The secret is to use a toaster oven, like this one. I know a lot of people who make their toasted cheese in a pan, with butter, and believe me, a sandwich made that way does not deserve to be called toasted, but only a sodden, greasy mess.

**Jeffery:**     Say, Madeline . . .

**Madeline:**    What?

**Jeffery:**     I was just wondering how things are going with you and Viktor these days.

**Madeline:**    Things are okay, Jeffery. Listen, you're not a bad person, but you and I are over. We had a time, and that's done. People move on. You can't stop progress any more than you can stop . . .

**Jeffery:**     Those sounds outside the Burrow late at night?

**Madeline:**    Actually that's not what I had in mind. I was going to say something like, well, the process of digestion—you know—once it's gotten started. Although those sounds you talk about . . . I do hear them, but really, they don't bother me all that much.

**Jeffery:** I see.

**Madeline:** Yes, Jeffery, I mean it's over between the two of us, and the sooner you accept it, the better.

**Jeffery:** Still, I don't understand you. First it was me, then Raymond, then Viktor. Don't you care about how many hearts you break along the way?

**Madeline:** That heart business is entirely up to you. Here's your toasted cheese. I'm taking mine back to my room. Nothing personal, Jeffery. I just feel like being alone right now.

■

Trisha Reed is having one of those days. To start with, immediately after her pre-newscast shower, while she is still at home, there is no way she can find the brand-new stick of antiperspirant she bought just the day before, and by the time she quits looking and leaves for the station it's too late to stop at the store for a new one—not that she's

worried about smelling bad—this is television, after all—
but television also means it's hot beneath the lights, and
all she needs is a couple of dark circles starting to spread
under her arms in the course of the show, and people will
start to talk about medical problems and addictions and
so forth. Besides, is it entirely too much to ask that the
highly paid supposed professionals in charge of doing
makeup might keep an extra stick of roll-on in their
bags for times such as this? Apparently it is. The result
being that she's stuffed a couple of wads of Kleenex in her
armpits and is about to go on air in ten. It's humiliating.

That's Number One. Number Two, the yellow high-
lighter she likes to use to mark the words of phrases in
the script she'll need to punch up when she reads them
is missing. The pink one is gone too, and so she's forced
to use a plain old ballpoint pen that has the name of
a dry cleaner on it, and the result is her script looks
like one of those books you check out from the library
where some lunatic has gotten there ahead of you and
has underlined various words or phrases—never the
ones she would underline herself—the result being that
her script looks like it was marked up by a psycho.

And speaking of psycho, Number Three comes when
she has just finished underlining her script with the ballpoint and Jessica, the intern, hands her a fan letter that is

supposed to cheer her up because Jessica is always doing extra things like this, having apparently misread her job description on the Intern's Code, or whatever they make them sign, which is just to do what the fuck you are told to, and now, instead of cheering her up, the letter turns out to be from some guy who claims he is a *fellow television personality* (underlined in ballpoint!), somebody who says that once upon a time he starred in some obscure sitcom in the ancient past and is now saying that she, Trisha Reed, reminds him of somebody or another he once worked with—the man is practically incoherent— but the upshot is that he says he wants to take her out and teach her how to "string his bow." Ugh, ugh, ugh.

"If you ever *ever* see another letter like this, destroy it," she tells Jessica. Then, Number Four, finally there's her cameraman, Fred, or Ned, or Jed, or Ted—that's how well she knows him—a large and balding individual who has just whispered seconds before she's going on air that he'd like to take her out for coffee, nothing more, he claims. "Just a chance to know you better"—in a pig's eye, she thinks—but on the other hand it's not as simple as that because anyone at all who is familiar with the basics of television production understands that camera angles can make or break your career, particularly on live TV, where there are no edits. And so now she has to figure out a way to tell whatever-his-name-is that this is not going to happen, but somehow do it in such a way that he doesn't take it personally. Men are such sick fucks.

"Good evening, this is Trisha Reed. On this evening's news we'll be talking about new sightings of people seen wandering around town who can't or won't respond to even the simplest of questions about what they are doing or why they are here."

■

There are two times Raymond misses Madeline the most. One is when he's looking at a newly arrived block of wood (wherever they come from), lost in thought trying to decide whether he should carve a teal, or a canvasback, or redhead, or mallard, or merganser, or even a wood duck, because back when they were together Madeline would come up quietly behind him at those very moments, run a hand through his hair, back to front, and ask, "What's it going to be, Big Boy?" and then, as if by magic, he would know *exactly* what it would be. The other is when he's up late at night, tired, just finishing the feathers on one wing or applying a coat of protective varnish to a completed decoy, because in those days Madeline was with him she would be lying there in bed waiting for him to finish, and then, after he'd finally washed his brushes, closed the last can of paint, and crawled in next to her, she'd say, "My God. The smell of polyurethane turns me on."

And Raymond has to admit he also misses how Madeline used to worry about whether he was getting enough to eat, or was eating the right foods, because now, if she cared to ask—which obviously she does not—he scarcely has an appetite. Still, because she is responsible for practically all the meals in the Burrow, he forces himself to eat although his heart breaks with every chew. He also misses the way she used to make him wear shoes around the apartment instead of just his socks, and he still wears them in her memory. But most of all Raymond misses the afternoons or evenings they'd be lying together in bed watching a nature special about ducks, and he would point out something the so-called experts had gotten wrong, or bring up something they had forgotten, and Madeline would rub his chest and say, "Oh Raymond, you certainly are an idiot savant." Then she'd explain, though she'd told him a million times before, that was French for genius.

And it *has* occurred to Raymond that, even taking into account his recent weight loss, he could easily beat

Viktor to a pulp and reclaim Madeline, because Viktor must be seriously out of shape, with the possible exception of what Madeline used to call the "love muscle," after being in front of a computer all hours of the day and night. Also, Raymond outweighs the man by at least fifty pounds, but anyway, except for causing Viktor pain, he's not sure what else violence would accomplish. In the first place, he knows those days of claiming a woman as your own are long gone. In the second place, Viktor was Madeline's idea, so if anyone claimed anything, she had claimed Viktor. In the third place, if he did something like that, he'd have to leave the Burrow. Not only does he not want that, but he doesn't even want to think about finding a new apartment, what with security deposits and first and last month's rent, and then having to move the decoys. In the fourth place, if he left he probably never would see Madeline again, and in the fifth place, after all, what kind of person would that show he is? Madeline left Jeffery to be with him, and afterward Jeffery was never anything but nice.

Is Madeline one of those women he has heard about who can't be satisfied by any man, but keeps on trying? Or maybe she's like a comet, and he's due for another visit.

Sometimes, walking by Heather's room late at night he can hear Heather talking on her phone to some distant boyfriend of hers, just a word here and a word there, but what she says makes Raymond blush.

*What would it be like to have someone talk to him that way?*

*Or to touch him?*

■

Episode One, *The Burrow*, Scene Six

The kitchen. EVERYONE is seated around the kitchen table and each person demonstrates different degrees of impatience. Some tap their fingers, others inspect their nails, yet others rub their thumbs against one another. The table is left unset, with its surface empty.

**Jeffery:**   I suppose you are wondering why I wanted all of us to get together tonight. I promise, I wouldn't take up your time if I didn't think it was very important.

**Madeline:**   Well, that makes me feel *a lot* better. So what do you have to tell us?

**Viktor:**   And make it fast. Some of us have work to do, you know.

**Jeffery:**   All right. Here it goes. I'll make it fast and simple. When was the last time any of us went out of the Burrow?

[silence]

**Heather:**    I remember the other day, I almost went out, but then something happened so I didn't.

**Madeline:**   The same thing happened to me. I was about to go out, I think to a place I know about that sells gourmet foods and spices, when somebody interrupted me just when I was about to turn the knob, so I wound up postponing it. Was it you, Jeffery?

**Viktor:**     It certainly wasn't me. Though I personally see no need to go out at all.

**Jeffery:**    Fair enough, but has it ever occurred to you that far from being satisfied tenants, we may be prisoners?

[general dismay]

**Jeffery:**    Think about it: Food arrives. Ray here gets chunks of wood and we have the Internet, but nobody goes anywhere. For all we know, we may as well be dead. And while we may not want to go out at the moment, someday we might, and I think it's better to know the situation now than when it's too late. Oh, and there's one other possibility I thought of as well. Are any of you hiding as a part of some kind of federal program? You can tell me. It will go no further.

**Madeline:** Jeffery, nobody here is hiding out from anything, but why don't you just walk yourself over to the door and try to open it. It can't be that hard.

**Jeffery:** As a matter of fact, I did try, and more than once, and every time something came up to make me change my mind. I mean, I started with the full intention of walking out that door, and all of a sudden I was doing something else. It's like I have no control over my actions at all when it comes to that door.

**Viktor:** So why did you ask us here? Was it just to tell us about your problem? What's the point?

RAYMOND stands as if he's going to leave, then sits back down again.

**Jeffery:**   It's simple. Here's what I thought: Just to be sure I'm not making all this up, I thought that if we all walked to the door together, we could all go outside, and then, if anybody wanted to, they could turn around and go back inside again. I mean—we wouldn't really have to leave the Burrow. It would just be a way to prove to ourselves that we can leave if we want to, and we would wind up feeling better.

**Viktor:**   You mean *you* would wind up feeling better.

**Heather:**   But suppose, if we are under some sort of spell or something, that once we left we couldn't get back inside.

**Raymond:**   Suppose I walked out, leaving all my decoys, and then I couldn't get back to them again.

RAYMOND starts to stand, but JEFFERY pushes him gently down.

**Madeline:**   Sit, Raymond. Actually, Jeffery, you have a point. If we are under some kind of spell—which I doubt—it would be better to know about it before it's too late.

Why don't we try Jeffery's idea, but when we go to the door, everyone should bring along the one thing they can't do without. That way, if somehow we *are* locked out for some reason, we'll be together, and at least we wouldn't be starting everything over again from scratch.

**Jeffery:**     That sounds fair enough. Heather, would that make you feel better?

**Heather:**    I could do that. It wouldn't have to be for long, would it?

**Jeffery:**     Raymond?

**Raymond:**   If everybody else is doing it, okay.

**Jeffery:**     Viktor?

**Viktor:**      I don't know. Let me think about it. But maybe.

**Jeffery:**     All right. Let's go back to our rooms and get the one thing that's most important to us. We'll meet at the door in fifteen minutes.

■

From the *St. Nils Eagle*

"Dead May Not Be Completely Dead, Scientists Claim"

Researchers from the University of Applied Medicine announced today that the dead might well be taking longer to die than previously thought. Even after a person is buried, university scientists report, it may take a dead person weeks, possibly years, to complete a process that in the past was believed to take only minutes.

"This is a complicated area," stated Dr. Carlton Bates, head of the university's Mortality Project, "and one relatively new to science. It may have to do with certain preservatives in food, or even household chemicals in current use, or the effects of modern drugs, such as multispectrum antibiotics. On the other hand, it may be as simple as the vast advances we have made in devices to measure deadness, what we like to call Mortality Meters."

Bates explained that though a person may well appear to be dead, and for all intents and purposes *is* "dead," the only way to tell for certain would be to interview that person, something that is currently not within the range of our capabilities. It could well be, he added, that for them nothing has changed in their lives in the least. He elaborated, "It may be that it's time to use words less absolute than either 'dead' or 'alive' to describe various states of existence." Instead,

Bates proposed what he called a "Living Quotient," which would have a built-in range, say, of 1 to 100, with 100 standing for "most alive" and 1 for "least alive." Anything lower than that, would, of course, be dead, he concluded.

In a related development, Dr. Rajish Chandrapanir, a researcher in the field of neuromnemonics at the university's pioneering Electromagnetic Imaging Department, was quoted as saying, "We have long known that we can stimulate memories in living brains through the application of localized electric current. There is every reason to believe the same techniques will work on the dead as well. The problem is only in determining exactly which memories, out of all those available, are to be accessed." He explained that researchers in this field are especially interested in what he called "Separation Issues," that is, learning how to preserve the most important memories and, at the same time, to leave behind 99.9 percent of the others, which he called "essentially worthless." Dr. Chandrapanir concluded that this whole reevaluation of what he described as "the old life/death conundrum" could seriously challenge our current measures of longevity and, in the long run, threaten the assumptions inherent in many social programs.

"The bottom line for you television and movie buffs out there," he said, "is that this has nothing to do with what is popularly known as a zombie. This is real."

■

*Tocar.*

■

"Hello. Hello. Who's there? Old Stag Killer—is that you?"

" . . ."

"Well, of course I'm startled. I never in a million years would have thought an inanimate object, let alone a crossbow such as yourself, would have the power of speech, but, hey, I'm open to ideas."

" . . ."

"Okay, so what's that you're saying? That the taste for blood has somehow been awakened in you after all these years, and now that you are awake, that you crave more?"

" . . ."

"Kill? And if I get caught, then I'm supposed to say that my crossbow made me do it?"

" . . . "

"All right, so I don't plan to be caught, but even if I entertained your crazy idea, who would you like me to take out?"

" . . . "

"Well, I have to admit, that does make a kind of sense."

■

Dear Members of the Cast of *Mellow Valley*,

You don't know me. I realize that your excellent show has been over for many years now, but still I am writing in the hopes that someone at this studio or maybe the station or the person in the mailroom will know how to find you, and pass this letter on so you can accept my sincere thanks for everything you did in putting on your show, because watching your show changed my life.

Do you remember (of course you must) the episode where Sergeant Moody finds the duck egg that has been abandoned because the coyote ate its parents so he takes it inside and keeps it warm? And then, when the egg hatches, how it thinks that Sergeant Moody is its mother, and follows him around, including trailing him into town, where bad people try to harm the baby duck and how the Sergeant uses the skills he learned in the Special Forces to save it, putting twelve of the townspeople, including a boy who was the same age as I was when I first saw this episode, which was eight, into the hospital?

So one of the reasons I am writing is to let you know I would *never* have tried to hurt that baby duck, either then or now. But even more than that, it was the selfless courage of Sergeant Moody that inspired me to spend my life making statues of ducks so people can take their time to admire them by keeping them in their living rooms or dens in order to truly realize how beautiful they are. Therefore, as a token of my gratitude, if you will send me your address, or PO Box, I would like to send each of you one of my duck statues, or decoys as some prefer to call them, to keep in your own homes, or maybe your star trailers. My name is Raymond, and my business is called Raymond's Decoys, so if you get this letter and would like to have such a statue, you can contact me c/o the Burrow in St. Nils.

Very truly yours, your friend,

Raymond

P.S. Every day I pray they bring your show back in reruns.

■

Somewhere in a city a man in a beret slowly shuffles forward. He wears a blue cardigan sweater and brown bedroom slippers, and his name, a thought that only occurs to him those times he least expects it—as when ascending a curb or catching his reflection in the window of a pet shop or a bakery—is Louis.

Louis is neither hungry nor not hungry. If he stares at the window of a bakery it is not so much with long-ing for the cakes and pies behind the glass, for the plates of cookies and trays of sweet rolls on display, as with the memory, long buried, of longing. If he pauses before the window of a pet shop to smile at the winsome kittens or to admire the determined hamsters on their wheels, it is not so much out of a longing for companionship as his half-remembering some distant time he cannot define precisely, when he must have been lonely, and back then—whenever it was—wouldn't it have been a comfort to have a hamster or some other small rodent he could carry in his pocket as a friend? Yes.

And so he trudges on. At times his eyes fill with dust and particles of abrasive grit, and without think-ing, he'll reach up and rub them until they feel better. At other times almost miraculously he is able to see objects far in the distance, to describe them as if they were only an arm's length away. Then that passes too before he has the chance to remember if this ever happened before, or if *this* is the first time and it only seems as if it happened earlier.

But the fact is, at this point he has no idea where he's going, and he has no idea how he came to be here. When he is thirsty, he finds a public fountain and bends down to drink. When he is sleepy he finds a bench and lies on it, or spots a relatively flat area beneath a bush and stretches out to nap, and when he wakes again he is curiously unrefreshed, his thoughts as hazy as ever. When it is hot, he unbuttons his cardigan. When it is cold, he buttons it—that's the nice thing about a cardigan, he thinks—but beyond that thought he does not care about the weather or the clothes he wears or anything that is not present at that moment. Whenever that moment actually is. *Wherever.*

■

Actually, Ballerina Mouse takes dance lessons only for a short time—maybe two, three lessons at most—then quits because she's no dummy. It doesn't take her long to figure out that a mouse with one foot turned practically in the opposite direction of the other is never going to be a prima anything. So, okay, she thinks. It's not in the cards, no matter what my name is, just like the fact that every boy who happens to be named Roy or Rex isn't going to grow up to be a king, either. As a result she spends the rest of her life pursuing something not very interesting, some sitting-down job, a clerk at a government office or reading to blind mice, and every year her foot twists a bit more, almost as if it has a life of its own, until by the time she's fifty in mouse years, she needs one of those aluminum platforms on wheels to roll in front of her to keep her from toppling into a gutter. Anyway, things go on that way for a while, and then, because getting back and forth to work is just too tough, she takes early retirement. Ballerina Mouse—a name she has almost forgotten by now, it having been replaced by her original one, Wendy—doesn't have family or any real friends, and the years—mouse years—pass: sixty, sixty-five, seventy.

Then one morning in her bed she doesn't move at all, not her good foot, not her bad one, which by then is truly, horribly bad, and has turned *completely* in the other direction and is actually on its way to coming back around the other side if she could only live another seventy years, which she can't because she's dead.

But in heaven, to her surprise—and she finds this out almost immediately—guess what! Her crippled foot is perfect, and she can dance and dance and dance straight through eternity, without ever missing a day, and so she does.

Oh, Ballerina Mouse, you were named correctly after all!

*Yes.*

*Maybe.*

■

*Suppose, just suppose,* the Captain thinks, one day there is a knock on the door of my luxurious home and when I get up to answer it, whom should I see there but my son—or at least one of them—who somehow managed to scrape up the money for an economy ticket, or maybe stowed away in the wheel well of a jetliner, or worked his way on a cattle boat, to track me down. And there he is, this young adult, wearing his cheap suit or inexpensive loincloth, and carrying a cardboard suitcase, or a backpack. What will I do? Will I invite him in and offer him a cup of coffee before I send him on his way again? Will he want to tell me the story of his life? Of course he will, and I'll listen. But after it's over, after he has finally finished, and he has picked up his suitcase or backpack to go back to wherever it was he came from in the first place, what exactly will his story have to do with me? How will his story be different than the story of any stranger, any random visitor to town who just happens to be passing through, or an actor, mindlessly reciting a part written for him by someone else? And, for that matter, come to think of it, what do the stories I tell have to do with all the reverential dolts who hear them and believe that, having made them a part of their memories, they will become better people for having heard them?

■

Episode One, *The Burrow*, Scene Seven

All the residents of the Burrow stand at the front door, which is a heavy-looking brown slab with numerous bolts and a large brass handle. No one dares to make a move, but MADELINE holds a recipe file, and JEF-FERY has a copy of his script, still in progress, tucked under his arm. RAYMOND cradles the decoy of a red-head duck, while VIKTOR clutches a CD that, according to MADELINE, contains a list of his bank accounts.

He also has a sock filled with marbles. HEATHER holds a music box with a ballerina on top. It's empty, but it's the place she imagines one day she will hide her most precious object in, as soon as it comes along.

**Jeffery:** Is everyone ready? This shouldn't take long, and then we'll know.

**Viktor:** Come on! It's taken too long already. Let's get it over with. I don't have all day. I have other things to do.

VIKTOR strides to the door and turns the knob. Then he stops, a look of puzzlement on his face.

**Viktor:** It looks like it's stuck.

**Jeffery:** Okay. So let's see.

JEFFERY walks to the door, turns the knob, and pushes his shoulder against it. He pulls it toward him, just to be sure, but there is nothing happening in that direction, either.

**Jeffery:** It *is* stuck. Raymond, you want to come over and give us a hand here?

RAYMOND gives his decoy to MADELINE to hold and runs at the door, hitting it with his shoulder. It doesn't move. All of them, even HEATHER, begin to push against it, but the door remains shut.

**Madeline:**   My Lord. I didn't think it was possible, but you may be right, Jeffery! I heard you, but, honestly, I didn't think there was a chance in hell that something like this could be happening. So what are we going to do now?

**Jeffery:**   I wish I knew. Let me think. Wait. Whoever or whatever is keeping us here is also bringing us food, and dropping off those chunks of wood for Raymond to carve, right? So it must mean they don't hate us. But it must also mean there has to be a way into the Burrow besides this door.

**Madeline:**   Yes, that's it? Somewhere there *must* be an extra door, maybe one that's hidden. That's what we have to find!

**Heather:**   But where do we start to look? It can't be in one of our rooms, or someone would have noticed people coming and going. Can anyone think of a place where there isn't some-

one hanging around 24/7, a place where a
person could enter and exit unnoticed?

Everyone looks at one another, each coming to the exact
same conclusion.

**All:**        The kitchen.

∎

The Captain stands in his kitchen, preparing a fruit
smoothie with some bran for extra fiber to help regulate
his bowels, when suddenly the image of that young
man in the lumberjack shirt, the one who brought up
that stupid *Mellow Valley* incident, pops unbidden into
his mind—Plaidman. *What is his game?* The Captain
wonders. The man looked familiar in a way. Could
he be the son of some old shipmate, or possibly the
jealous boyfriend of one of those women who were
having such a pleasant time taking a shower together
on that day until the rest of the cast and the police with
their unnecessarily wailing sirens burst into that idyllic
moment? Did Heather have a boyfriend he hadn't heard
about? Could such a person still be out for revenge
after all those years? If so, why hasn't the man surfaced

earlier? Is it possible that he has become permanently unhinged by grief after being spurned by Heather, and this is his pathetic attempt to worm his way back into her favor? Or, deranged from the very beginning, the man's mental illness had been held in check by one or more stays in a hospital for the criminally insane and liberal doses of psychotropic medication, but now that he's been released, he is out for blood and he doesn't care whom he strikes?

On the other hand, could this young-appearing man be part of the same plot that was set in motion by those unnamed intelligence agencies so long ago, the ones bent on embarrassing him regarding the women, the same ones who might well be digging holes in his front lawn? Is Plaidman as young as he seems, or has his appearance been altered through cosmetic surgery—and actual cosmetics as well—to throw the Captain off his guard? Is the beard part of a disguise? Damage Control, he remembers they called it back in the days of tradecraft. Is the man an agent? Or, for that matter, suppose the man is the son of one of his old enemies, possibly the Swede, or the Ukrainian, who, disposed of long ago off Trieste, now seeks to avenge his father?

The Captain feels his Death Quotient rising again, and in a way, it feels good.

■

<u>Episode One, *The Burrow*, Scene Eight</u>

EVERYONE is gathered in the kitchen once again, but this time no one is sitting; no one is fidgeting. They stand in a rough circle around the kitchen table.

**Madeline:** So here we are. Where do we start?

**Jeffery:** Well, I've never been in a situation like this, but why don't we all start looking for a secret door or passage. Okay, everybody start by checking the cabinets. Maybe one of them has a door or hallway behind it that leads to the outside world.

There is a flurry of door openings and closings, and often the same door is opened and shut two or three times, as people forget what's been checked and what hasn't. In the midst of all of this, RAYMOND stands unmoving.

**Viktor:** Nothing. Not a thing.

RAYMOND walks absently to the stove and turns on the burners.

| | |
|---|---|
| **Viktor:** | There won't be anything there, for Christ's sake. That's a stove. Why are you turning on the stove? What the fuck are you doing, Duck Man? Have you lost your mind? |
| **Madeline:** | Duck Man? Is that what you think? You watch yourself, Viktor. |

RAYMOND stands where he is and begins to open and close the oven door of the stove, as if listening for something. He repeats this several times.

| | |
|---|---|
| **Viktor:** | For Christ's sake. |
| **Raymond:** | There's a draft. |
| **Heather:** | A what? |
| **Raymond:** | A draft. There's a draft coming from the stove. |
| **Jeffery:** | Let's see. |

JEFFERY walks to the stove and feels above and below it. Then he puts his fingers to the side of the mirror above and behind the stove, and the mirror swings open, on hinges like a door's, exposing a large hole in the wall behind it. The hole is about two feet high, and maybe three feet wide.

**Jeffery:** Mystery solved.

**Madeline:** So what do you want to do?

**Jeffery:** What do you mean? I'd say we don't have a choice. Obviously this tunnel, or whatever it is, leads somewhere. Even if we decide to come back, we'd better see where it goes before we figure out for sure if we're trapped or not. This could be a dead end.

**Viktor:** Maybe one of you should explore it.

**Madeline:** What do you mean, "one of you"? I say we all stick together. It's our only chance.

**Viktor:** I meant one of *you*. Listen, I don't need to explain myself to you, and I'm certainly not afraid, or anything like that. I just changed my mind, that's all. I'm staying. Whatever you find out has nothing to do with me. I have my work to do; unlike the rest of you, I have a business to maintain.

VIKTOR begins to stuff his hands into his pockets, then thinks better of it.

**Viktor:** You all can do what you want. I'm not going anywhere. That's it. It's final. I'm staying here.

**Jeffery:**     Suit yourself. Are you still in, Madeline?

MADELINE nods.

**Jeffery:**     I'll lead, and the rest of you can follow one
                 by one. Raymond, you go last, just in case
                 anybody tries to stop us. See you around,
                 Viktor.

**Heather:**     But suppose it's dangerous? Suppose
                 something happens?

**Jeffery:**     What could happen? Anyway, remember
                 to prop the door open, and we can always
                 come back here again.

**Raymond:**     Don't worry, Heather. I'll be right there
                 behind you.

∎

Meanwhile, it so happens that Junior's old theatrical
agent, a man of dubious character whom Junior hasn't
seen in years, has sent him a letter now resting in the
young actor-turned-psycho's mailbox, waiting to be read.
In this letter his agent says that amazingly, against all
odds, *Mellow Valley* has finally been picked up as a rerun
in one of those ex-republics of the former Soviet Union.

There will be translation issues, of course, he adds, but it's a sign of how desperate for new material the networks are these days. In any case, Junior will be receiving at least a little money for this, minus, of course, the twenty percent that he, as Junior's agent, will be taking. Oh, and beyond all these matters concerning business, he hopes Junior is well and prospering in whatever new career he's found for himself. Yours truly, etc. etc.

But Junior isn't near his mailbox, or even at home right now. He's doing something else.

■

Reruns. That's a good one. Ha ha ha.

■

Junior crouches behind the rosebush, watching the window of the luxurious home, practically a mansion he guesses you could call it. Soon it will be dark, and then ...

But wait! Is there something there? He thinks there could be, so he gets Old Stag Killer ready. It was no problem at all getting over the wall, and then finding the perfect place to hide was easy too. He laughs—ha, ha—because now he is no more than thirty yards from the house. Does the man have dogs? He could take them out, but it seems there are no dogs. Excellent. Better yet.

Then there is a movement at the window, and is it? Yes . . . it's his father . . . no, the Captain . . . no, his father . . . no, the Captain . . . but who cares, really? This is who he came for, and anyway, father or not, this is the man who has come to assume the role of father, or close enough, in Junior's tortured and confused mind, the same man who used to call him Junior on the set of *Mellow Valley* as if it wasn't his real name but a joke, so that even as far back as the days of *Mellow Valley* this strange ironic vibe had been set in place, and anytime anybody anywhere said "Junior" they were referring not only to him, Junior, but at the same time making a sinister inference about his television character as well, and also to the Captain's being Senior, which could not help but make a complete mockery of his position in the hierarchy of the production so after that there was no way in a thousand years he could have asked Heather for a date, which was what he had been planning to do before the old shithead snuck up on her and Judy and got some kind of eyeful. It made him glad that he had switched those signs around.

"I hate you," Junior says under his breath. He raises Old Stag Killer to his shoulder and looks through the crossbow's sight.

Now the man is outside, and holding something, possibly a cup of coffee in a grayish mug, peering out at his lawn, not seeing Junior at all, not having the remotest idea of what's in store for him, but admiring, no doubt, the perfection of his stupid perfect grass. My fucking father, he thinks, lost in admiration for his lawn and not for his son, who deserves it. It isn't fair at all. He cocks Old Stag Killer, but wait—the man has turned away and—Junior's sight line is blocked by a bush—seems to be heading back inside, maybe to get something he's forgotten.

*Come back*, Junior thinks. *And soon.*

■

*To touch.*

■

And so they know this much: that there is a tunnel, and that they are in it, but nothing more than that: not what will become of them, nor where they are headed—only that in the distance there is—what?—a light, and then perhaps a dark, and then possibly a light, and so on, but still they are there, wherever *there* is, and possessing a being that is theirs nonetheless, a being with no name and that has no reason, nor can it make any clear distinction between what is and what is not—a being, if it can even be called such, that sees only chance and dimness and regret, a *something* that hears only the muffled sounds of wave after wave, the grinding sounds of pebbles on a beach; an unnameable sound; an unnameable taste; a soul—well, who knows, and who can say?—but if there is one, it is—whatever it is—half-formed, unshapely, half-light, half-dark— as if, it thinks, *if I only had the chance to learn a little more, to study a little more, had time enough to prepare, to brace myself, then*—each of these things, whatever we may call them, thinks—*if only just a little—then I would have understood whatever it was I needed to know, the part that was to be found in me, the part that I could never quite encompass, before the light goes completely out.*

■

It's totally amazing, Madeline thinks as she's standing there waiting her turn to crawl into the hole that will take them out of there, or somewhere: all this time she's been considering Jeffery pretty much a loser (and he *is* a loser), and yet he's the one who came up with this plan to get them out of there. And even though earlier she hadn't been so sure she really wanted to go outdoors—because what is out there except the clouds and a lot of nameless trees?—now that it's so close, so nearly happening, she's excited.

And Madeline can just about taste it: first a little restaurant with cheap rent because it's off the beaten path somewhere, then a couple of excellent reviews from food critics, one, two, three stars, long lines, guest appearances on television, her own show, a book—or maybe the book will come earlier, when she still will have the time in her schedule to write one and every spare minute isn't taken up by the demands of celebrity because who needs Viktor?

She gets up on the stove, scraping her knee on one of the burners, and crawls into the dark. *Cooking with Madeline.* Here she comes.

■

Raymond is still holding his decoy, which is impossible to see in the dark, but feels safe and friendly, like a real duck, almost.

■

*But come to think of it*, Jeffery thinks, *this Burrow script doesn't sound like a first episode at all. It sounds like a last one.*

■

Heather, sensing the dark shape of Raymond behind her, relaxes.

■

And between having touched without knowing it, and thinking you have touched but having not touched at all, what is the difference?

■

It's twilight and the Captain hears outside his window the slow grinding of machinery, but when he looks it's impossible to see a thing. Still he hears it. Something must be there, he thinks—so he steps outside the house onto his beautiful lawn, where he still sees nothing, but now that he's outdoors he can feel the low vibration of the earth beneath his feet. And then all at once, it becomes clear to him; he puts two and two together.

He knows exactly what's about to happen. He returns to the house, picks up his old pistol, the faithful, blue-black Walther, right where he left it, and, pulling a chair up to his window, rests the pistol's butt on the windowsill to steady it and waits for the first movement on the surface of his yet unbroken lawn. He remembers something an old Malaysian hunter once told him: "When you take aim, you must not see the tiger you are shooting, or the deer, or the bear, because to take the life of a living thing is difficult. Instead you must imagine that the tiger, or the deer, or whatever" (the hunter didn't say "whatever," of course) "does not exist at all, but in its place is only a single burning candle, and it is your task, and yours alone, to direct your bullet safely through its flame to the other side."

The hunter's name was Old Robert, or something that sounded like that. It will come back to him, he's sure, but all at once and out of nowhere he's suddenly become very sleepy.

He yawns and touches the anchor-shaped birth-mark above his left eye for good luck. That's better. A Quotient of eighty-five, maybe ninety. The Captain is all together ready for whatever is going to pop out of his lawn—a gopher, bear, or who-knows-what.

■

And everything does come back.

■

Now at the far end of the lawn, over by the wall that Junior found so easy to climb over, patient tendrils of plants push out of the soil like fingers, each searching for a grasp, a hold, a thing to cling to, to pull themselves up, for the hundredth, for the thousandth, for the millionth time, toward the light.

■

And it *does* come back, doesn't it?

■

That is: Not the thing, but the representation of the thing. Not the passion, but passion's show; not emotion, but the memory of once having experienced the emotion; not life, but a half-life, a representation of a life, one set out by someone or something, possibly higher, probably not, but certainly *other*, though for what purpose it's not possible to name, not possible to summarize—only that intention does not count, or desire, or tragedy, or comedy, but instead some unnameable other, some word still unspoken, unthought of by anyone since the very beginning of words, the most important word of all, which is, at the same time, perfectly and totally irrelevant to anything that ever was thought, or could be thought, no matter when.

■

And why, if the dead only dream that they are living, should they want to wake? Why should they want to come back, to spread out once again, like a stain?

■

*To rerun.*

■

Which is not the correct word at all, by the way.

■

To touch.

■

To participate.

■

*But in what?*

■

Not that it matters.

# Acknowledgments

Thanks to the early readers of this book: Lee Montgomery, Janice Shapiro, Dylan Landis, Monona Wali, and also to my wife, Jenny, and our son, Henry, all of whose responses were invaluable. I am amazingly fortunate to have Meg Storey as my editor; her care and thoughtful annotations to each draft are reflected on every page. Special gratitude to Julie Starrett for her permission to use Michael Woodcock's painting *St. Joseph's Day* for this book's cover.

JIM KRUSOE is the author of the novels *Parsifal*, *Toward You*, *Erased*, *Girl Factory*, and *Iceland*; two collections of stories; and five books of poetry. He is the recipient of fellowships from the National Endowment for the Arts and the Lila Wallace Reader's Digest Fund. He teaches at Santa Monica College and lives in Los Angeles.